The
FLINT HEART

The
FLINT
HEART
A Fairy Story

Freely Abridged from
Eden Phillpotts's 1910 Fantasy

by Katherine *and* John Paterson
illustrated by John Rocco

CANDLEWICK PRESS

First paperback edition in this format 2018

The Library of Congress has cataloged the hardcover edition as follows:

Paterson, John (John Barstow)
The flint heart / by John and Katherine Paterson ;
illustrations by John Rocco. — 1st ed.
p.   cm.
"Freely abridged from Eden Phillpotts's 1910 fantasy."
Summary: A magical amulet brings power
and despair to those who touch it.
ISBN 978-0-7636-4712-4 (hardcover)
[1. Fairy tales.]   I. Paterson, Katherine. II. Rocco, John, ill.
III. Phillpotts, Eden, 1862–1960. Flint heart. IV. Title.
PZ8.P273Fl 2011
[Fic] — dc22   2010048225

ISBN 978-0-7636-6243-1 (paperback)
ISBN 978-1-5362-0371-4 (digest paperback)

19 20 21 22 23 TSH 10 9 8 7 6 5 4 3 2

Printed in Dexter, MI, U.S.A.

This book was typeset in Manticore.
The illustrations were done in graphite and colored digitally.

Candlewick Press
99 Dover Street
Somerville, Massachusetts 02144

visit us at www.candlewick.com

To Steven *and* Helen Kellogg
with gratitude for a magical friendship
and for
our dear Margaret Mahy,
who introduced us to the original story

K. P. & J. P.

To Victor *and* Anita

J. R.

The universe is full of magical things,
patiently waiting for our wits
to grow sharper.

—EDEN PHILLPOTTS, 1862–1960

Contents

Fum Makes the Charm

⌒⌒ Many years ago, oh, let's say five thousand, more or less, there lived in the south of England, in what is called Dartmoor, tribes of people who had never thought to make anything out of metal, much less plastic. They had stone houses, stone spear tips, stone axes, and stone arrowheads. They raised the biggest stones in circles and lines and squares and all sorts of formations that nobody today quite understands the meaning of, and maybe they didn't either. If you are one of those people that think people in those long-off days were much kinder and gentler than people are today, you are being far too romantic. Of course they didn't have guns or tanks or airplanes, but there were plenty of rocks lying around, and when one tribe wanted to have a war with another tribe, they threw rocks at each other, always trying to see who could throw the biggest lump at his enemy. You have probably already guessed that the time these ancient people lived in is now called the Stone Age. The Stone Agers lived in tribes on the moor, a landscape of rocky hills and lowlands of peat and swamp. It was not a great place for farming, which they hadn't invented anyway. The rivers that ran through the moor teemed with fish, and there was plenty of wildlife, in addition to the sheep and cattle that the tribes raised. So the people ate fish and meat and, using the bones for needles, made clothes out of the animal skins.

In the tribe, which mostly lived in the little rock village of Grimspound, there were two very important people. The first and most important was the chief of the tribe, a great warrior whose proper name was Brokotockotick, but because that was a long name (and if you'd never heard of cuckoo clocks, really hard to pronounce), his subjects called him Brok behind his back. The second important person was the tribe's mystery man, who lived a short way outside the village. He didn't have a fancy name; he was simply called Fum, which nobody had trouble pronouncing. Fum, despite his simple name, was sort of a combination of Lord Chancellor and Lord

Chief Justice. He was also the only doctor in the village and the Poet Laureate. This meant that whenever the chief had a birthday or won a battle or his wife had a new baby, Fum was called upon to compose a song to celebrate the occasion. Since writing had yet to be invented, Fum had to make up these songs in his head and sing them by memory, which was no mean trick as some of them ran to two hundred verses or more. (At this point, we need to make note of the fact that although Fum was the most famous singer of his day, he was not by any means the first. Actually, the first Stone Ager who sang made everybody jump. In fact, he seemed so amazing and wonderful, so unlike everybody else, that they took him out to the top of a high hill and chopped his head off with a flint ax—just for a warning to other people not to be too clever. Fortunately, by the time Fum came along, people no longer killed off artists, unless they were simply too dreadful to endure.)

In addition to his civic and cultural duties, Fum also fashioned things from flint—arrowheads and spearheads and other useful items. But the thing about Fum that made him a mystery man was his uncanny ability to make charms out of flint to frighten off the Bugaboos who lived in the swamp. He claimed that these charms were very difficult to make and that he could only make them when the Thunder Spirit was with him. (People thought this was wonderfully mysterious, but it was actually just clever advertising. Fum had seen the Thunder Spirit only once or twice and would just as soon never see him again.) There was no money yet, so people who wanted a charm paid for it with a live sheep, and if they wanted an extra-strong charm, they would have to bring two sheep.

One day Fum was trying to make a flint brooch, which Chief Brokotokotick wanted to give his wife for a present, but the work wasn't going well. He'd already ruined several perfectly good pieces of flint when a young warrior named Phuttphutt appeared at his doorway, which was really only a piece of hide hanging from the rock ledge above the entrance to his rock workshop.

"You're supposed to be the wise man of the tribe," Phuttphutt said, without as much as a how-de-do. "I want to know why it is that Brok is chief of this tribe and not me."

Fum was so startled that the rock hammer in his hand slipped and shattered yet another piece of flint. "What do you mean, Phutt?" (Everyone called the young warrior

"Phutt," both in front of his face and behind his back.)

"You remember that in our last great battle I killed fourteen men and wounded ten more."

"Of course I remember," said Fum. "You may recall that I composed quite a handsome song to celebrate the fact."

"Then perhaps you remember also that when the survivors ran for their lives, I was the one who took a white moleskin war waistcoat from the body of the chief and a silver fox petticoat that belonged to the dead chief's wife."

"Quite true," said Fum.

"Well, tell me, then: who wears them now?"

"Why, Mr. and Mrs. Brokotockotick wear them," said Fum.

"Exactly. Brok took them from me. Indeed, he grabbed all the best things and left the second best for me. He claimed it was his right. And what I want to know is why."

"Because he is stronger than you."

"Nonsense," said Phutt. "I am stronger, I am younger, and my muscles are bigger. I belong to the Order of the Grey Heron Feather, just as he does." (Here he indicated the grey heron feather stuck behind his ear, which was the only thing he wore besides his bearskin. The feather was awarded only to warriors who'd killed more than fifty enemies, so Phutt was quite proud of belonging to the Order of the G.H.F.) "In the last battle," Phutt continued, "he killed only seven men and a boy. That shows I'm a better warrior than old Brok."

"Hmm," said Fum. "Maybe a better warrior, but not a stronger man. He's got a more powerful will. He was born to rule; you were not. If you want to be at the top of the tree in this tribe, you've got to be as hard-hearted as a wolf. That's where he beats you, my boy. You're too soft."

Phutt considered this for a moment. "You're right," he said. "So what you must make me is a charm that will give me a hard heart—the harder the better."

"Hmm," Fum said, "it can be done, but you'd better think about it."

"If it can be done, just do it," said Phutt.

Fum shook his head. "If I make you such a charm, there'll be no more peace in the tribe until you are chief."

"If your charm is strong enough that won't take long. You know how hard Brok's heart is. You only have to make mine twice as hard and—"

"There's something else," Fum said. "It's

true you'll be chief, but you'll lose the affection of the tribe. Brok is headman, but he's not the favorite man. They don't shout for him as they do for you. The children don't weave garlands of foxgloves for him, nor do the women make him necklaces of wolves' teeth, as they do for you."

"Bah!" cried Phutt. "Who wants children bothering 'round him or necklaces of wolves' teeth? I want my white moleskin war waistcoat and power . . . unlimited power!"

Like the best mystery men, Fum was a lover of peace, so he tried to change Phutt's mind, but to no avail. Finally, he thought of a way out of the difficulty.

"As a matter of fact," Fum said, "such a charm would be frightfully expensive."

"How expensive?" asked the warrior.

"Oh, far more than you could afford," said Fum, thinking he had solved the problem.

"How much?" Phutt demanded.

I have to make the cost ridiculously high, thought Fum, and so he said, "Thirty-two sheep and thirty-two lambs," heaving a sigh of relief, for he felt sure that Phutt would never pay—even if he could— such a price as that.

Phutt looked very thoughtful, so Fum went on, "What's the good of a hard heart, my boy? A soft heart wins much more pleasant things. And to be head of a tribe like this isn't a bowl of whortleberries. I've got an idea. I'll make you a fine charm for catching white moles. You'll catch so many that soon your wife will be able to make you a white mole-skin war waistcoat that will fit you better than that old thing the chief is wearing; besides,

I've heard that the moths have gotten into it and it's no longer . . ."

But Phutt wasn't listening. "This charm will make my heart twice as hard as Brok's?" he asked.

"It will, and so you'll have twice as many difficulties as Brok."

"And I'll be twice as able to deal with them."

With this, Fum gave up trying to influence the stubborn warrior, who went home to count his sheep and lambs. It turned out that he had exactly thirty-two sheep and thirty-two lambs. His total flock was just enough to pay for the promised charm. So the delighted Phutt went to see the mystery man the very next day.

"But that is your entire flock!" said Fum. "You won't have anything left."

"You're not as clever as you pretend to be," said Phutt. "When my heart turns hard, I'll have as many sheep as I want. Cows, too. Anything I want, for that matter. Now, when shall I have the charm?"

Fum sighed. "In a month—if all goes well. But you have to understand, flint is a tricky stone—you never know if it will split the way you intend."

"I'll be back in a month," said Phutt. "And when you hand me the charm, my thirty-two sheep and thirty-two lambs will be driven into your fold."

Off he went, and Fum took a stone, planning to give it a few trial whacks, when an amazing thing happened. At the first blow, the flint split into three pieces, the center of which was a bright black heart with a hole right through it. Fum was astounded. He had earned thirty-two sheep and thirty-two lambs with one blow of his ax. It gave him a very eerie feeling. He knew that such a thing did not happen by chance. It could only mean that the great, dreaded, and mischievous Thunder Spirit had helped him. His first impulse was to throw the Flint Heart into the river, but

the Thunder Spirit might swoop down and burn him to a crisp if he were to do that. (It had happened once long ago to a mystery man named Sminth who had had the nerve to quarrel with the Thunder Spirit. All that was left of Sminth was a bit of charcoal about the size of a coconut.)

There was nothing for Fum to do but go to his doorway and call to Phutt, who was still within earshot.

You can imagine how surprised Phutt was to see the Flint Heart. He hadn't been gone a minute. He couldn't help but feel that Fum had cheated him out of thirty-two sheep and thirty-two lambs, and he didn't hesitate to say so.

"You may take it or leave it," Fum replied. "And frankly I'd rather you'd leave it. As sure as my name is Fum, you're going to regret it if you don't."

"We'll see," said Phutt. He strung the Flint Heart on a leather boot string, hung it around his neck, and, went to look at himself in the pond outside Fum's doorway. But instead of his own reflection in the water, he was alarmed to see the face of a dark and terrible phantom staring back at him. The phantom wasn't ugly, but it was strange, with eyes the copper color of the sky before a storm. Its hair was rose and blue and a dazzling flame color; it twisted and tangled over the phantom's forehead in a fury of fire. Phutt staggered back from the reflection, only to see above him in the sky the terrifying shape that had thrown its image into the pond.

"Look!" Fum said, racing out his doorway

and pointing. "The Spirit of the Thunder! Listen. It speaks!"

And out of the sky came a peal of many thunders. The awful music rattled and roared across the horizon. The rocky hills caught the noise and flung it backward and forward among them.

"Now you've done it," said Fum. "I wouldn't be you for all the sheep in Dartmoor."

But after the first shock, Phutt recovered and smiled and nodded. "That's enough, Thunder Spirit," he called to the sky. "We're not deaf, you know."

Fum's mouth dropped open. How dare Phutt be rude to the Spirit of the Thunder? He expected to see the arrogant warrior reduced to a lump of charcoal, but apparently, the Thunder Spirit rather enjoyed the spectacle of a human bug who dared to talk in such a sassy manner. It broke out into a peal of laughter that made the very ground shake, then, gathering up its garments, swept away through the storm.

In a moment the sky turned blue again, but not nearly so blue as Fum, who went back into his workshop to tackle the brooch for Mrs. Brokotockotick. Meanwhile, Phutt hurried toward Grimspound, eager to test out his new powers.

The Reign of Phutt

It so happened that at the entrance to the main rock wall that ran all around Grimspound, three children were sitting in the road playing knucklebones. When they saw the great and beloved warrior Phutt approaching, they called to him, "Come play knucklebones with us, Mr. Phutt!"

"Get out of my way!" shouted Phutt, and before the startled children had time to move, he gave a mighty kick and sent them flying in three directions.

A woman who witnessed this terrible sight went screaming into the village. "The great warrior Phutt has gone mad!" she cried. "He's killing the children at the gate!"

The father of the children, who thought, of course, that his children were dead, went rushing out and began cursing Phutt with the strongest words in the tribal language, such as *spzfluta* and *bbjkfjiuk* and even *bubblexg*—none of which, fortunately, we can still pronounce today. When the distraught father had finished sputtering his curses, Phutt coolly took out his flint-headed ax and whacked the man on the head, killing him on the spot.

Consequently, people hesitated to disagree with Phutt. To question his judgment meant a broken jaw or a dig in the stomach. Those unwise enough to openly argue with Phutt found their heads split down the middle before they could take their hats off.

Mrs. Phutt, like a proper wife, sided with her husband, but the thirteen little Phutts howled if he looked at them and ran for protection to the great, lean wolfish sheepdogs that guarded the flocks by night. But once Phutt had had a word with the sheepdogs, even they turned cowardly, and the moment they heard his voice, they bristled and growled and skulked away with their tails between their legs.

After about three days of this, the tribe waited until they were sure Phutt had gone off bear hunting and then sent a delegation to Brok to beg that, in the interest of peace and progress, the head of Phutt be removed from his shoulders as quickly as possible.

Naturally, Fum was chosen to speak for the delegation, but he rather garbled the petition, for, like everybody else, the mystery man was terrified that Phutt would return before any plans could be made. He was stuttering and panting as he described all the kickings and jaw breakings and stomach diggings, not to mention downright killings, that Phutt had committed.

"Take a breath," said the chief. "There is no hurry, my dear Fum. I am disengaged until suppertime." Which shows what a wise, considerate, and reasonable person Brok was for those days.

Fum thanked him and continued: "We therefore beg, implore, beseech, and also pray that it may please your cheerful and kind-hearted Amiability to stand between us and the awful severity of Phutt—"

"He's coming, he's coming!" cried the others, who had kept their eyes nervously on the gate.

"The sooner he comes, the better," said Brok. "We are greatly annoyed. It is quite wrong and not at all nice. Don't we have plenty of enemies if he wants to go around killing people? I don't approve of this loose way we have fallen into of killing one another without a proper reason. It isn't gentlemanly, and it sets a poor example for the children. What's more, I won't have it. Tell Phuttphutt to come here at once."

"I regret to say that he won't be ordered," Fum said. "Only yesterday two courageous people tactfully hinted to Phutt that his conduct threw him open to criticism. He replied by chopping them in two."

"Then it is time for us to act," said Brok.

He rose off his granite throne, hitched his white rabbit-tail-trimmed bearskin robe about him, and put on his kingfisher feather crown. "Phutt must be cautioned," he said sternly, "and if it happens again, he shall be punished."

The chief called for his Chair of State, and four of his warriors carried him on it to Phutt's door, with the entire population of Grimspound trailing behind to see what would happen.

They found Phutt standing in his doorway eating a piece of cake, while behind him in his rock house Mrs. Phutt skinned the bear that he had brought home on his shoulders.

"Good afternoon, Phutt," said Brok.

"Afternoon," said Phutt, with his mouth full.

"You're having your tea, I observe," said the chief politely.

"You observe right," answered Phutt.

"Does it occur to you that a great many brave men would also be having their tea at this moment if you had not slain them?"

"Pooh!" said Phutt. "Don't be sentimental." And he went right on eating his cake.

There followed a long, painful silence, during which you could have heard anybody wink.

Finally Brok climbed down from his chair and, staring right into Phutt's face, said, "Look here, Phutt. Am I your chief, or am I not?"

"You are not," answered Phutt.

"Then I accuse you of treason," said Brok, who was beginning to lose patience, "and you know what the punishment for *that* is."

"That is neither here nor there," said Phutt. "What I say is that I deny your right as chieftain of this clan and claim it for myself."

"Perhaps you'll tell me why," said Brok.

"Because I'm stronger and bigger and younger and a better manager than you," said Phutt.

"You may be," answered Brok, "though I'm not prepared to admit all that. But, as I am chief, and these gentlemen and ladies are perfectly satisfied with the way I and my wife manage things, it ill becomes you to talk this nonsense. You are in the minority of one."

"So be it," said Phutt. "Then who will join the minority?"

No one said a word, and the fearsome Phutt spit on his hands and took up his battle-ax.

"If you won't all join the minority, then you shall all join the majority!" he cried, and with this dreadful threat he shouted at the Spirit of the Thunder to lend him a hand

and boldly attacked the entire tribe. His first blow laid Brokotockotick dead at his feet, and though the Thunder Spirit didn't actually kill anybody, it rattled and roared a good bit and made it clear that it was all for a change.

So the rest of the warriors surrendered without any further unpleasantness because their wives begged them to on behalf of their children, and besides, Phutt promised them all a present on the occasion of his next birthday. Then Phutt put on the bearskin with rabbit tails and the kingfisher crown and everybody bowed down before him and asked what his first order as chief was going to be.

As it turned out, Phutt's first order was to build a funeral pyre and burn Brok's body on top of it. There was to be a splendid funeral, at which Fum was to compose a funeral song long enough to last over three days. As was the custom at the time of sudden death, Brok's ashes were to be carried miles and miles away from Grimspound and buried under a huge pile of rocks. (This was so that his ghost would get lost in the middle of the moor and not by any chance find his way back home.) "Then I shall ascend the granite throne and we will rejoice for a month and eat and drink day and night until we nearly burst ourselves. And after that we shall want some hard work and exercise, so I shall lead you against all our enemies."

So Phutt reigned instead of Brok, and we don't want to go into all the terrible things he did, because they were too awful to speak of. He won all his battles, and everyone in the tribe did exactly as he told them to, though they hated the ground he walked on. Poor Mrs. Phutt was so unhappy that she died, but

Phutt didn't care. He married twenty-seven other wives and bullied them all. Among his other deeds was the destruction of all the Bugaboos, except for one that he kept on a chain to frighten the children. He caused the tribe to become the fiercest, most cruel, most powerful tribe in Dartmoor, but despite all their riches and power, their new roads and chimneys, and the fact that Phutt invented farming and declared lots of holidays, nobody liked him because he ruled entirely by fear. And to be always frightened gets on people's nerves after a while.

So, despite all his triumphs and splendor, Phutt was a cloudy and careworn man. Sometimes he looked back a bit nostalgically on those days when he had a soft heart, but he never really considered going back. As he grew old, he clung to his terrible Flint Heart and was sure that no future chief of his tribe would be able to get along without it. So he summoned Fum and made him promise that he would hand the Flint Heart on to a certain grandson whom Phutt had chosen to succeed him.

Fum promised to do so, but he didn't keep his promise. When the ashes of Phutt were taken far out on the moor for burial, and while everyone was distracted by the lengthy verses that Fum was singing to commemorate the solemn occasion, the mystery man secretly dropped the Flint Heart in among the chief's ashes, and it was buried along with Phutt under hundreds and hundreds of rocks. For Fum knew the awful harm that it could do and wished it to disappear forever.

And here, for five thousand or so years, we leave the terrible Flint Heart resting deep in the bosom of the moor.

The Jagos of
Merripit Farm

Thousands of years have passed, and now
we find ourselves in the England of one hundred years ago. As you can well imagine, there
have been some changes in Dartmoor. The
Stone Age village of Grimspound is just a pile
of old rocks. Over the stone cairn under which
Phutt was buried grows a great mound of the
toughest, prickliest gorse in all of Dartmoor.

And no wonder. Its roots are down in the dust of that tough and prickly tyrant.

However, two of the main characters from long ago are as lively as ever. One is the Thunder Spirit, who still rattles and roars just as he did in the good old days of the Stone Age, and the other is the Flint Heart. Fum buried it to keep it out of mischief, and it has been kept out of mischief ever since, but unluckily, it has not turned to dust, as Phutt has. But if you were able to ask it how it was doing down there, it would probably say, *Doing quite nicely, thank you. Thoroughly rested and perfectly ready to begin business at once.*

On top of the ground, tucked under the hills and beside the sparkling rivers, there are farms and cottages. Even the pigs and cows have nicer homes than the Stone Agers of our earlier chapters. One of those homes is called

Merripit Farm, and it lies just a few miles from poor old ruined Grimspound.

Long before Merripit Farm was established, however, Dartmoor was discovered by the pixies.

Some of you who are modern and scientifically minded will say you don't believe in pixies or fairies or any of their relatives, like the brownies and trolls and flibbertigibbets and dwarfs and pigwidgeons and spooks and ghouls, etc., etc. But you'll have to take our word for it, because this story will not make any sense at all if you don't believe in pixies and other so-called fantastic creatures, as you soon will see.

But let's turn our eyes now to Merripit Farm, where they are having a wonderful dinner. It's Christmas Day, so you can just imagine how good it is. They began with goose and went on to a plum pudding and mince pies and finished up with ten oranges and ten sticks of the best milk chocolate and ten puppets made to represent Father Christmas. The puppets' heads screwed off and they were full of mixed sweets.

At the head of the table sits the father, Billy Jago, a big man with a red neck and pale hair and a fat, clean-shaved, good-natured face. His wife is named Sally, and his children are John, who is eighteen and very grown up; Mary, who is fifteen and a great help to her mother; Teddy, whose only gift is fishing for trout; and Frank, who can imitate ducks and turkeys and fowls very well, not that it was much use. But more important to our story is twelve-year-old Charles, who nobody took seriously except Unity and the baby, even though he was a great reader and probably had more

brains than any of them. (To be honest, however, most of his reading was done in the Boys'
First-Rate Pocket Library, whose one-penny
books featured two of his great literary heroes,
Deadwood Dick and Fred Fearnot.) Next come
the twins, Sarah and Jane, who never speak,
then Unity, who is only five and who, like all
proper five-year-olds, is always surprised. She
begins almost every sentence with "I wonder,"
which is quite a contrast to John, who at eighteen tries hard not to be astonished by anything. Oh, we almost forgot Baby Dicky, but
he, of course, is there as well. And Ship, the
family sheepdog — we mustn't leave him out.
He was bigger than the baby, with very shaggy
black and white hair that fell right over his
eyes. His tail had never been cropped short, as
Charles had begged his father not to do such
a cruel thing to a defenseless puppy, and Billy

Jago had agreed, not having much appetite for the operation himself. You won't be surprised to know that ever since that day Ship had felt especially fond of Charles.

Now that you've met the whole family, we can go on with the story. It was in the middle of this most pleasant of Christmas dinners that Billy Jago made a most astonishing announcement.

"Up along by Fur Tor, I was riding along on the pony, looking for the foal Nat Slocombe lost, and I fell in with a stranger. He was a lean slip of a chap, long in the legs with a learned-looking nose built for poking into things. Seems he's terrible interested in the old stones stuck up on the moor. And he offered me ten pound—ten pound!—if I'll do a job for him up on top of Fur Tor."

"Ten pound, Father!" cried Mrs. Jago,

and all the little Jagos echoed, "Ten pound, Father!" All except John, who, as previously mentioned, was not astonished at anything, owing to his age.

"Yes," said Mr. Jago, "but I'm very much afraid he might as safely offered me a hundred, for 'tis doubtful I can do it. In a word, he says there ought to be bronze hid in some of the old graves up on the moor. And if I dig up a bit, he'll give me the money."

"'Tis a wild-goose chase," declared Mrs. Jago, "and well you know it. The last learned fool as come up here six months digging and delving — what did he find? Some ashes, a few odd bits of broken crockery, and three amber beads — which you could buy in Plymouth for tuppence. You'd best mind your own business, Billy."

Mr. Jago took a card out of his pocket.

"The gentleman's name be Nicodemus Nestor Frodsham Perke, F.R.S., British Museum," he said.

"Well, let him go perk somewhere else," said Mrs. Jago. "Us haven't got no use for him."

"Of course, I ban't a-going to waste my time with the man," said Mr. Jago, "but since tomorrow's a holiday and there's naught for me to do, I shall just help him a bit. That old grave as he've found under Fur Tor have never been broke open by the look of it, and nobody but him would have found it, for 'tis right in the midst of the prickliest fuzz bush as ever I comed across. But tomorrow I be going to break it open—just for to see if anything be there. And no harm's done since the day be a holiday."

"More fool you," said Mrs. Jago.

But when the next day came, Mr. Billy put on his working clothes and went. Charles, being the most sensible of the children, went with him to help carry his furze hook and pick and spade and basket, and Ship went along, too, just for the fun.

They reached the spot, but there was no professor to be seen. He had meant to be there, but on the way he had come upon a most interesting location and sat down to contemplate it. By and by he had filled three notebooks with ideas for a new book that would explain in a new way how Dartmoor came to be, and he was so excited by these new ideas that he stayed there too long, caught a cold, and went back to the inn to recover, recalling never once his appointment with Billy Jago.

Meanwhile, Charles and his father began to cut through the furzes and hack away at the peat and heather. They dislodged the stones and eventually threw open the old grave. Since it was old Phutt's grave and he was a Stone Ager, they didn't find any bronze there, and it would have been better if they had found nothing at all, but Billy did find something, which he slipped into his pocket. "The gentleman might like this here funny old stone," he said.

"'Tis just a piece of flint, Father," said Charles.

"Of course 'tis — any fool can see that." And his father, who was usually such a kindly man, spoke so roughly that Charles backed away in astonishment. But you won't be surprised, because you've already guessed that the Flint Heart in Billy Jago's waistcoat pocket was bubbling away with wickedness, delighted to be at work again.

If Charles had happened to look to the southwest at that moment, he would have seen the Thunder Spirit laughing over the edge of a black cloud. But Charles was staring at his father and missed the sight. Billy loaded his pipe, lighted it, and then said to his son, "Pick up the tools and carry 'em home."

"All of them, Father?"

"Yes, all of 'em. You heard me. You ain't deaf, are you?" Then he strode off, leaving Charles almost as still as the granite stones of Phutt's grave. Soon the boy's astonishment turned to tears, because he loved his father exceedingly and was grieved to see him so suddenly changed. Then he dried his eyes, got the tools together, and with Ship dragging the pick along in his teeth, the two of them started for home.

They made slow progress, lugging all that gear, and it was dark before they got home to Merripit, but it could not be called merry anymore, for the Flint Heart had arrived and set to work at once.

When Charles came in, he found his mother pacing the kitchen in a rage and John sitting by the fire, nursing a black eye and try-ing not to look astonished. Mary was getting the twins to bed; Teddy was under the table, shivering with fear; Frank was hiding behind the storage bench; Unity was wondering; and the baby was sound asleep. His mother turned to Charles at once.

"It's all the fault of that wretch of a man — no doubt," she said. "I suppose he've made his ten pounds, and now he feels too grand and fine for his own home and his wife and children."

"Do please give me something to eat," said Charles. "I'm terrible hungry. Father left me to drag home all the tools, and if it weren't for Ship, I should never have made it."

"Who was this here man?" his mother asked as she got him something to eat. "I should think 'twas Old Scratch himself from the way your father's going on. He's bewitched — so sure's I'm alive."

"Nobody came near us," said Charles with his mouth full. "We dug and dug and found nothing but a bit of flint with a hole in it. And then, sudden as a flash of lightning, Father turned on me and spoke as he never spoke afore and ordered me to bring home all the tools and went off without me. By the looks of you all, he wasn't no better when he got back."

"He come shouting out for his dinner," Teddy said, "and when Mother said 'twasn't ready, he said it ought to be. Then John stood up for Mother, and Father knocked him edgewise over the fender. Just look at his eye! Then Frank and I ran out, 'cause we thought it would be our turn next. When we come back, he and Mother was having a pretty set-to, wasn't you, Mother?"

"I think he's gone mad — or else the pixies are having a game with him," said Charles.

"As a rule," said Teddy, "when Mother and Father have words, Mother gets the best of it. Don't you, Mother? Only this time, Father got the best of it. He ate up all the tidbits of dinner, and then he went off because he said he wanted to pluck a crow with Mr. French, down in the valley. He said he didn't see why Mr. French should be the leading man in Postbridge, and he wasn't going to stand it. Goodness knows what'll happen next."

At that very moment a terrible noise broke out down by the garden gate. Men were shouting and dogs were barking. Then there was a crash, and Ship ran out to see who the dogs were and Charles ran out to see who the men were. Mrs. Jago stayed where she was, as did John and the rest of the children. They had been so terrified already that they felt it didn't much matter what happened. Mrs. Jago sighed and John asked for another piece of brown paper for his eye.

Then the master of the house came in, followed by Charles.

He was quite pleased, was Mr. Jago, but he didn't show pleasure in the old and kindly fashion. He stomped in and slapped his leg and declared that he'd done a good stroke of business. "I met old Bassett going down the road, and I offered him a bit more for that field of his than French offered, and now I've got me a rich meadow that I've been wanting for many a day. When I met French and told him what I'd done, he got into a proper rage and hit me, so I gave him one on the head and rolled him over in the hedge."

After that Mr. Jago called for his supper and didn't strike anybody, nor did he talk to anybody but John. He seemed to have forgotten that he had given John that black eye. He talked about the future as if he and John were the best of friends.

"We'll soon wake this place up!" he said. "If we get to work and harden our hearts against all their nonsense, we'll come out at the top of them all by this time next year. I know how to get the best of them, and John's going to help."

Then he explained to John a number of horrid ideas that had occurred to him. They were not exactly the sort of ideas that had occurred to Phutt when he had the Flint Heart, because the world had moved on a good deal since Phutt's time, and among other things that had come into it were policemen. Policemen have quite spoiled a good many fine and dashing deeds people used to do because they interfere and march you off to prison, and there's nothing in the least fine or dashing about being locked up. But Billy Jago knew all about policemen, and he planned his future accordingly. There are all sorts of dodges in business, and Billy Jago, who was once such an honest and straight and kindhearted man, seemed now not only to have learned every one of these abominable dodges but also to have become horribly clever at putting them into practice — in the course of which, he made enemies of everyone for miles around.

At home, Billy gradually grew a little calmer. Even the Flint Heart occasionally got tired, and in those moments, Billy relaxed and laughed among his children and was quite the amiable father he had once been. But these moments passed all too quickly, and then he behaved in a fierce and savage manner once again.

At last the children and Ship held a meeting in the wood house to determine what to do about their father. John was not invited, because it looked as though he was going to imitate Billy. Charles took charge. "Brothers and Sisters and Ship," he said solemnly, "we have assembled here to find some way to make Father nice again."

And all of the children answered, "Hear, hear!"

Frank stood up to address the meeting. "Father's a regular right-down beast."

"Order! Order!" said Charles. "The question before the meeting is how to make him nice again. You'll hurt Ship's feelings if you call Father a beast."

Frank sat down and Teddy stood up. "Let's give him a present," he said.

"Hear, hear!" said all the children.

Then Mary said, "Where are we to get a present from?"

Charles asked everyone for ideas, and they all—except the twins, who never spoke—made speeches, until at last it was Unity's turn.

"I wonder," said Unity, "if big brother Charles had not better go to the pixies for Father's present."

And all the children said, "Hear, hear!"

And Ship barked something that seemed to mean "Hear, hear!" as well.

"I think," said Charles, "that Unity has made the cleverest and most practical speech of the meeting. I will do my best," he said to them. "We've none of us ever seen a pixie, but we all know very well that there are such people. Tomorrow evening I'll go alone to the Pixies' Holt. I hope I may have the luck to see one and speak to him. And if he'll be so good as to listen, something may come of it."

With that the meeting broke up, but not before Mary had proposed a vote of thanks to Charles for chairing the meeting and for what he had promised to do.

MR. DE QUINCEY

༼༷ Months had passed since that terrible day
when Mr. Jago had dug up the Flint Heart, so
it was already spring when Charles went to the
pixies' hole, hoping to meet a pixie. He found
himself in a little wooded dell, knee-deep in
bluebells with great moss-covered rocks towering above him. There was a tiny hole between
two of the rocks, and that was the entrance, so
people said, to the fairy city. Charles sat down

among the bluebells and waited patiently for a pixie to appear.

At length, his patience was rewarded. A tiny brown thing emerged from the hole. At first Charles mistook it for a weasel or a stoat, but when it stood up on two legs and stretched its arms out, Charles could see that it was a tiny man with thin cheeks and a forehead larger than the whole rest of his face. The pixie had grey whiskers and a sharp nose. He wore a long cloak, belted at the waist, with a hood of dead-fern color, which ended in a point over one ear. Under his arm was a tiny book.

The pixie stood on tiptoe and smelled a bluebell. Then he sniffed the air like a little mouse out for adventure. At length he sat down on a blade of grass, sighed, put on a tiny pair of spectacles, and opened his tiny book.

Now, as we know, Charles loved books, and he also knew how hard it was to leave them once you got started. So he thought he'd better speak before the pixie began to read and get interested. So he stood, bowed politely, and said, "If you please, sir, may I talk to you?"

The pixie looked up, as we would look up at the sky when it thunders, and without speaking drew out a tiny telescope and examined Charles from head to toe.

Finally he said, "You are a human boy, I see." His voice was thin and sharp, like the sound made by the wings of a fly, but he spoke distinctly and Charles heard him very well.

"Yes," he answered. "I'm twelve and my name is Charles."

"Any relation to the *great* Charles?"

"D'you mean King Charles?"

"No," said the pixie, "I do not. I mean Charles Dickens. For practical purposes, in the history of England there is only one Charles."

"I'm afraid not," said Charles. "I never heard of him."

"So much the worse for you," said the pixie, and he turned back to his book and began to read.

"The question is," Charles said, "if I may have a few words on a sad subject."

"There is only one sad subject," the pixie said. "And I am always quite ready to discuss it. But first let me reduce you to a more convenient size. Have no fear. When our talk is at an end, I will restore you to your original dimensions."

Though Charles was puzzled by this speech, he felt no fear. The pixie took a pencil from his pocket, drew a diagram on Charles's shoe, said a few magic words, and in an instant Charles found himself on a level with the little fairy man.

"Now," said the pixie, "put yourself at ease and we will discuss the saddest subject in the world. First, let me say that my chosen name is De Quincey."

"Do fairies choose their own names?" asked Charles.

"Certainly. Why not? At twenty-one, when we are called upon to give ourselves a name, the great name of De Quincey had not been appropriated, so I chose it. Which brings me to the saddest subject in the world. I refer to the music of English prose. It is gone. We have lost it. The music of prose is a thing of the past." Here he took out his handkerchief. He was evidently going to cry.

"Don't cry—explain," said Charles. "I don't know what you mean by the music of prose."

"For that you must read the great English writers," he said, "those who are immortal banners on the topmost turret and battlement of our glorious mother tongue!"

"Dear me," said Charles. "How beautifully you talk. I do wish I understood these things."

"Nobody," said De Quincey, "can ever say that I do not sustain the charms and cadences of the language. If I ask for another cup of tea at breakfast, it is done like an artist. But"—and here he sighed deeply—"I am not appreciated. Who cares for the music of English prose nowadays? Nobody—nobody. And that is the saddest thing—the only sad thing in the world."

"Was Shakespeare anybody much?" asked

Charles. One summer some people had stayed at Merripit, and one of them had left behind a copy of *A Midsummer Night's Dream*.

"Take off your hat when you mention that name!" ordered the fairy, and Charles did so immediately. De Quincey himself removed his brown hood, revealing a very bald head.

"Have you read his funny book about the pixies?" asked Charles.

"Before you were born or thought of," answered the fairy. "He visited Fairyland in order to write it. That was before my time, I grieve to say, though the stories of his various sojourneys among us remain a part of our glorious tradition. . . . But we are forgetting the music of English prose. The loss — the heartbreaking loss! It is a case for many and bitter tears." And here the little man began to truly weep. Charles noticed that each teardrop that rolled down either side of the fairy's nose was like a tiny seed pearl. They pattered and hopped on the ground as though they were hail, except they didn't melt.

"Can I have some of those beautiful tears?" Charles asked timidly.

"'Tears, idle tears, I know not what they mean,'" said De Quincey, seizing the chance to quote Tennyson. "Yes, yes, you can have them, but they will be of little use to you. The tears of fairies are the seed of the flower euphrasy—Milton, by the by, mentions this herb in *Paradise Lost*. Plant fairy tears, and euphrasy will spring up. Experiment has shown that my tears always come up purple."

After this there was a long silence, and Charles, who had a kind heart and liked to talk of things that he knew interested people, asked the pixie about the book he was reading, because he thought the pixie would be pleased to talk about it.

"The work I am perusing happens to be a dictionary," answered the fairy. "There is much pleasure and profit to be won from the pages of a dictionary. I have read and studied every letter of the alphabet—all but Z. You may have observed that I never use any word beginning with that letter. The reason is that I have not yet studied it."

"I know two words beginning with Z," said Charles.

"You surprise me. I should not have expected that. What are they?"

"Zebra and zany," answered Charles.

"Thank you. I have met the zebra within works of natural history," said De Quincey, "but *zany* is unfamiliar to me. What do you mean by it?"

"A chap who plays the clown—who's foolish."

"Capital," said the fairy. "I'm tired of calling the other fairies fools. Now I can call them *zanies* instead. It will make a nice change."

"I thought all fairies were as sharp as needles," said Charles, quite surprised by the idea of foolish fairies.

"Far from it. Society of all ranks consists mostly of fools. We people of brains—I include you because you know two words beginning with Z—we clever people have to think for those who can't think for themselves."

"How lucky I am," said Charles, "to have met such a wonderful, clever pixie, for if most of them are thickheaded, they couldn't have helped me. Now I'll tell you why I've come."

Then he told De Quincey about his father and how he had changed and how all the children (except John and including Ship) had held the meeting to decide what to do. "After we decided on a present, the question was, what should it be? Unity, our little sister who is five, suggested I should come and ask the pixies. And here I am."

De Quincey thought for a few moments. He didn't have the slightest idea what kind of present the Jago children should get for Billy Jago, but he pretended that he knew all about it.

"The problem is not difficult of solution," he said. "Many far more profound cases than this have come under my notice, and I have never had anybody find fault with my decisions. But it happens that next Tuesday

evening the Zagabog—a Z, by the way—
visits us. It will be a brilliant evening, with
music, recitations, dancing, and a dinner of
thirty-eight courses, dessert ices, and the best
of wines."

"That's all very interesting," said Charles,
"but I'm afraid it won't help me."

"It may or may not," said De Quincey.
"That rests with you. The Zagabog, of course,
knows everything. I suppose you were aware
of that?"

"I've never heard of him."

"And never heard of his Agent-in-Advance,
the Snick?"

"Never."

"Then I withdraw what I said about your
being a clever person," said the fairy.

"I'm very sorry," said Charles, "but it was
no good pretending I did if I didn't."

"Not a bit," De Quincy agreed. "The Zagabog is easily the best, most brilliant, and the wisest creature in the universe. What he doesn't know doesn't matter. Now I will tell you what I can do. Our leading statesmen, philosophers, and men of letters have each received permission to bring one guest to the banquet. You may come as my guest, and I have little or no doubt that the Zagabog, if I make a favor of it with the Snick, will answer your question."

"That is very kind, I'm sure. I don't know how to thank you, dear Mr. De Quincey," said Charles.

"You may have it in your power to do me a service on some future occasion," said the fairy. "It is not probable, because we move in very different walks of life, but the world is full of possibilities, so who knows? We shall expect you, then, at eight fifteen because the King will arrive at eight thirty. Be punctual, for the King is the soul of punctuality. It is his only strong point, between ourselves."

"I will be there, but it seems almost too much to have dinner with the King and the Zagabog and the Snick— and you."

"It is dazzling, no doubt, and a great experience for a human boy," agreed De Quincey. "You must not, of course, expect to be the guest of the evening. The Zagabog is the lion of the occasion. You will come merely as my friend. But I may tell you that any friend of mine will have a certain amount of attention paid to him."

"I hope not," said the boy. "I only want to sit in a corner and see it all. Or I might help with the dishes."

De Quincey was much annoyed at this.

"You must come in the spirit of a guest, not in the spirit of a footman," he said. "You must be as grand and haughty as you know how — out of compliment to me. I need hardly say that we dress for dinner."

"Of course," said Charles, "so do I."

"Indeed! Forgive me, but I should hardly have expected that you did."

"Always," said Charles, "and also for breakfast and supper."

De Quincey was quite impressed. He had always felt that dressing for dinner was a matter of pure convention. "Why dress for dinner if you don't dress for breakfast?"

"Why, indeed," said Charles.

"There is no explanation. I hope," said the fairy, "during the course of the banquet that you will take occasion to mention pretty loudly how you always dress for breakfast."

"Certainly, if you wish it," said Charles.

"It will show that you possess the priceless gift of originality and may add to your importance. Now, remember, when you arrive next Tuesday, my secretary will meet you here. I shall be too busy putting the finishing touches to the Ode. But the Secretary will be ready to reduce you to a reasonable size and conduct you into the entrance hall. Good day to you, now."

"And good afternoon to you, sir, and thank you, indeed, for all your kindness," said Charles. And gathering up the fairy's tears, he placed them in a bluebell.

Then De Quincey touched Charles's boot and said a magic word, and Charles shot up to his full height of five feet one inch. It felt quite dangerous to be so tall, and the fairy tears in the bluebell looked to his human eyes like the finest dust. When he got home, he sowed them in the garden and stuck a label over them that read MR. DE QUINCEY'S TEARS.

Then he called another meeting and told everybody all about the things he had seen and heard.

The Fairy Banquet

ᏔᎤ After Charles had told the meeting all about his adventures at the Pixies' Holt, Unity spoke to him privately.

"I wonder," she said, "if I might come to the fairies' party."

Charles explained that she hadn't been invited, but Unity didn't seem to think that mattered, and since Charles loved her very much, he agreed to take her.

"I wonder," she said, "if Ship might come as well."

Here Charles drew the line. "He could come and see us safely home afterward, but of course, he couldn't actually come to the party." So when Tuesday night arrived, Unity and Charles and Ship went off secretly to Pixies' Holt, arriving at eight fifteen, just as De Quincey had directed.

De Quincey's secretary proved to be a small, middle-aged fairy with a rather sad face, which is what happens to people who are long accustomed to doing exactly what they have been told to do. He worked the charm first on Charles, who found himself three and a half inches high, then on Unity, who found herself two and a half inches high, and then on Ship, who was much surprised to find himself an inch and a half high.

Then Unity said, "I wonder if Ship might come to the party now."

Ship didn't wonder at all but simply announced that he was coming. They understood what he said because once you are reduced to fairy size you are able, like the fairies, to understand all languages.

So Charles asked the Secretary, who said that as it was none of his business, he couldn't really say, but since there would be a great many important squirrels, several water voles, certain nice birds, and a hedgehog in attendance, he supposed one more creature could hardly make a difference. Then he led the way, and the three Jagos followed after.

Each bluebell at the entrance of the Pixies' Holt had a glowworm sitting on the top of it, so the visitors entered the vestibule through a glimmering avenue of lights. Inside they saw

a large gathering of fairies and other creatures all chatting and waiting for dinner to
be announced. The men fairies were in evening dress, which consisted of black-and-white
bean flowers, and the ladies wore gowns made
entirely of brilliantly colored flower petals.

De Quincey was running about in an
excited manner, and when he spotted Charles,
he came rushing over. He could not conceal his
astonishment when he realized that Charles
had brought two uninvited guests, but it was
clear that Unity had immediately made a great
impression on him, and indeed a little crowd
had already collected around her.

She looked very lovely and less raggedy
than usual because she and Charles
had taken care to wear their Sunday
clothes, but they realized at once

that even their best clothes did not please Mr. De Quincey. "This will never do," he said to Charles. "You must come with me. Convention demands a bean-flower costume on this occasion. As for your sister, the ladies will see to her." Then Charles was hurried off to De Quincey's house, where the Secretary found a bean-flower suit that fit him fairly well except under the arms, where it was a little tight. The fairy girls dressed Unity in a gown of blue speedwell petals that made her look delicious. As for Ship, he was not expected to dress, and the red ribbon already around his neck made him far more dressy than any of the other animals, who had merely combed their fur or feathers and washed their paws or claws, as the case might be.

Presently a gong sounded, and the guests

streamed into the banquet hall, which was bathed in a pink glow that added much to the natural beauty of the fairies, making the old look merely middle-aged and the middle-aged appear quite young again. Places were laid for 335 persons. The beasts sat at a table apart, but quite near enough to hear the songs and speeches. Ship sat between a lady stoat and a lady pheasant. They tried to look at life through one another's eyes and taught one another many things worth knowing.

Unity sat between De Quincey and Charles, and on Charles's left was a beautiful fairy named Lady Godiva. At the head of the table were the King and Queen with the Guest of the Evening, the Zagabog, between them. The King and Queen were elderly, but still handsome. The Zagabog was not merely elderly; he was as old as the earth itself. His friends were the Spirit of the Rain, the Spirit of Burning Mountains, the Thunder Spirit (whom we met earlier), and others equally important and powerful. But he was older than all the rest and also more wonderful and more wise. Indeed, he went around the world paying visits like this one, seeing where he could be useful and make people happier and wiser.

He wore nothing but gold and behaved in the kindliest manner to great and small. His table manners were unpretentious and he knew everything. Strictly speaking, he was not beautiful, except for his pale-green eyes. His back was round; his nose was large and long. His hands were really more like paws than hands, and his tail was ratty, but very neat and always well cared for.

The Snick really *looked* more remarkable than the Zagabog, though he was only an Agent-in-Advance. He wore a black suit covered with an academic gown and lots of medallions. He made a great deal of fuss about the Zagabog and pretended that his employer was booked up for years and years ahead, and he altogether behaved in such a way that you might have thought that *he* was the great man and the humble Zagabog was a mere nobody.

The banquet consisted of the best fairy food, which we will not describe here as it would only make you discontent with your own supper. You'd be wanting only to taste the magical dishes and drink the magical wine, which never goes to your head, only to your heart. So we will go on to the time when everybody had had enough, except a few of the beasts, who had had too much.

Then the Snick, who was Master of Ceremonies, stood up, wiped his mouth on a rose-leaf napkin, and rapped loudly on the table with the drumstick of a roasted grasshopper.

Everybody cheered him, and the Snick, who liked fame—even the fame that belongs to a mere Agent-in-Advance—bowed to the right and to the left and to the high table, where the royalty sat.

"Your Majesties, Mr. Zagabog, Ladies, Gentlemen, and Beasts, our entertainment this evening is various and picturesque, gorgeous and refined, harmonious and artistic. The first item will be an ode composed and written by the fairy poet De Quincey. It is entitled 'Mr. Zagabog,' and it will give you a brief sketch of the life history, achievements, and precious peculiarities of your honored guest."

There was a great stir. The Zagabog smiled out of his gentle green eyes and lifted his wineglass to Mr. De Quincey. There followed Mr. De Quincey's ode, which was actually more like a cantata than a poem, for it was set to music with soloists and chorus. The soprano called herself Madame Melba, and her voice was like the little twitter of the swallows when they are catching flies for their young. The high notes of the gentleman soloist sounded like a bee in a cowslip, only with more feeling.

You can't have the music and text of this great performance because of copyrights, etc., but you must believe me that this fine song of the history of the Zagabog was very much admired, and the Zagabog himself liked it as well as anybody. First he called up De Quincey and patted him on the back and

shook hands with him. Then the solo sing-
ers, the chorus, and the orchestra were all
brought up to be complimented. Everybody
agreed that it was quite the best song that De
Quincey had made. He himself got so excited
that Charles was afraid he would break down
and cry again, but De Quincey soon recovered, and, bowing to everybody, he returned
to his seat and dashed off a filbert shell of dry
aged whortleberry wine. He was then himself
once more and ready to criticize the next item
on the program.

Which was to be, the Snick announced, a
fairy story by Hans Christian Andersen. The
aged sprite who went by that most famous of
all names in all the Realms of Fairie got up,
waited for the applause to die down, sucked a
honeydew lozenge to steady his vocal cords,
cleared his throat, and began to recite with

all the ease and polish of a skilled storyteller a tale of "The Old Woman and the Tulips."

"In the days of Your Majesty's great-grandfather, we pixies had rather more to do with human beings than is at present the case. The deterioration of mortals set in about a hundred years ago, and it has steadily increased—"

At this point Charles was horrified to hear Unity interrupt the speaker. In her tiny but shrill voice she piped out, "I wonder if you would make it easier, please. I don't know what you are talking about."

Some fairies cried, "Hush! Hush!" and the Snick said, "Order!" while De Quincey was furious that any guest of his should be so rude. Charles was just about to apologize humbly for his sister, pleading her age, when the old fairy spoke.

"You are perfectly right," he said. "I stand corrected. Anybody who uses a word of more than three syllables in a fairy story doesn't know his business. It shan't occur again." And then he proceeded in simple but elegant language to tell of an old woman who, in the time of the present King's great-grandparents, grew lovely tulips in her garden because she knew how much fairies loved tulips. The fairies in

turn liked her so well that they used to churn her butter, clean her cottage, tend her bees — in short, do all those things that fairies can do for mortals, if mortals will only permit them. In exchange, the fairies had free use of the tulip beds in spring. It was a great event for the fairies when the tulips bloomed, because tulips were ideal cradles for pixie babies. During the day the blossoms opened wide, and the mother fairies would lay their babies in the warm blossoms and gently rock the stems. At night the blossoms would close tight, so no wandering rascal of a spider or beetle could blunder into them and frighten the babies, nor could rain fall on them if there was a shower.

Sadly, the old lady died. The next owner was a horrid young man who pulled up all the tulips, threw them into the river, and planted turnips. The fairies were so outraged that they made sure that every crop of turnips he planted was a failure. Indeed, nothing was allowed to grow on that land. He never tried tulips, and they were the only plants that the fairies would have permitted to prosper. "And the end of the story is that we"—he said "we" because Hans Christian Andersen was one of those very pixies—"always looked after her grave in gratitude to her memory. Never a weed grew there. Never a mole burrowed there, but the grass was always trim and neat, and a white violet was the sole flower that we allowed to grow upon it. And that is the end of my simple tale."

Then the old fairy bowed and sat down.

"A good enough story, but rather too sad for the occasion," said the King.

The Zagabog, however, thought very highly of it. He complimented Hans Christian

Andersen on his language, took wine with him, and hoped that the telling of the story had not made him too tired.

Everyone was happy to hear the Snick's next announcement, for he declared that the first half of the entertainment was concluded and that during the interval of fifteen minutes before the second half, refreshments would be served.

After intermission, there was a dance of 350 fairies, appearing in companies of fifty. The first company wore emeralds, and they glittered like dawn beating upon the foliage of the birches at the forest edge in springtime. The second company wore sapphires, and they shone like sunlight on the deep blue sea. The third company wore topaz, and they gleamed like honey through the comb. The fourth company wore rubies, and they sparkled like wine-red seaweed rippling through the fingers of the tide. The fifth company wore fire opals, and their loveliness was like that of a kingfisher twinkling beside a river. The sixth company wore sardonyx, and they moved in the tender light that comes at afterglow. The seventh company wore diamonds, and they blazed with the dazzle of lightning and the cold frosty fire of the fixed stars.

The dance wound and turned and twisted and frisked and frolicked and sank and sprang up again, splintering and mending and breaking into new figures until the eyes of Charles and Unity ached at so much amazing color. It continued for an hour, and when the glorious ballet of the jewels had come to its close in slow throbbing music, produced by ten basso frogs croaking in time and tune, each company parted from the next, taking the shape of a letter until the letters spelled out

ZAGABOG.

The Zagabog declared that in all his experience he had never seen any dance that pleased him better, and only a dozen or so that had pleased him as well. He congratulated the companies, the dancing master and mistress, the artist fairy who had designed the dresses, those who had made them, and, in fact, everybody concerned.

Then something happened that looked very unfortunate at first but turned out in the long run to be most fortunate indeed. Several fairies, gravely shaking their heads, whispered something to the Snick, whereupon he rose and made an announcement.

"Your Majesties, Mr. Zagabog, Ladies,

Gentlemen, and Beasts, our next item on the program, which was to have concluded our entertainment, cannot, I regret to say, take place. The famous insect tamer, Von Humbolt, had hoped to introduce his troupe of performing caterpillars to your notice, but owing to an unforeseen interference of Nature, his talented company have all turned into chrysalides during the night, and until they reappear in the shape of butterflies, which will not happen for a considerable time, he cannot give us a performance. He much regrets your natural disappointment, but as he very truly remarks, 'It can't be helped.'"

A sound of sorrow arose from the company, and some of the younger fairies even cried. But then the Zagabog beckoned to the Snick, and in a few moments the Snick addressed the company again.

"I am delighted to inform you that Mr. Zagabog himself has most generously and kindly consented to take the place of the performing caterpillars and tell us a story."

Immense cheering greeted this good news. The Zagabog winked his sea-green eyes thoughtfully once or twice and then began his tale.

The Zagabog's Story

༄ "When I tell you I am going to relate 'The True Story of the Hare and the Tortoise,'" began the Zagabog, "I know quite well what you'll say. You'll say, 'We've heard it before,' but you haven't. However, sometimes even the youngest of us make mistakes, and so I'll forgive you all. The true story is quite different from the one you know, and the moral is quite different. If you also tell me that you don't want to hear a story with a moral, then I can only beg you to excuse me this once, because I am rather old-fashioned and in my young days we had morals to all our stories. But you can easily forget the moral again after you've heard it. It isn't an uncomfortable moral, and in fact, it wouldn't hurt a fly.

"Now, first I must ask you to consider the subject of points. There are the points of mountains, points of tacks, points of jokes, and so on. But there are two points more important than any of these; one we all have, and one we all ought to have. The point we all have is the point of our noses, and the point that we all ought to have is the Point of View. The Point of View is the most important of all points, and everybody should have his own in the first place, and everybody should be very tender to everybody else's Point of View in the second place, because a Point of View is always a tender thing.

"Which admirable reflection brings me to the true story of the hare and the tortoise. The hare was a jovial, rollicking chap and full of fun. He did not think much of his own powers and was always ready to credit other people with more skill and cleverness than he himself possessed. He had a good sense of humor, as modest people often have, and he enjoyed a joke as well as anybody. Also he had a kind heart and a good store of sympathy for other creatures, and the creature with which he most sympathized was the tortoise. He was always cheering up the tortoise, praising his good points, admiring the pattern of his shell, and so on. Sometimes he would stop from his own gambols for half an hour at a time just to talk with the tortoise or put a little furniture polish on his back or bring him some delicacy that grew too far away for the tortoise to reach it himself.

"On the other hand, the tortoise, I am sorry to say, was not a sympathetic character. He had been badly brought up. He took narrow views of life and was jealous and rather given to seeing the worst of people instead of the best. His real, good qualities he hid carefully, instead parading silly little tricks and habits. He had some wrong opinions and was rather bad form altogether. One of his wrongest opinions centered on the notion that he could run. This, of course, was just the thing of all others that he could not do. If he had said that he was a champion sleeper, nobody would have doubted it, for he could tuck himself up in his own shell and go to sleep for six months. That was rather wonderful, and he

had a right to be proud of it. But like a good
many other people who scorn their own sort
of cleverness and claim another sort that they
haven't got, the tortoise thought nothing of
his great sleeping talents; however, he crawled
about at the rate of a yard an hour and said
that not the fox nor the hare nor the antelope
nor the greyhound could keep up with him if
he really hurried.

"He quite believed this himself. You must
give him credit for that. It seemed to him, as
he waddled along, putting down each leg as
slowly as the minute hand of a grandfather
clock, that he was going at a fearful rate of
speed. He had often passed a snail or a slug,
so he concluded that he was rattling along
quicker than a motorcar, and when people
chaffed him about it, he thought they were
jealous and got sulky and drew his head

into his shell, refusing to come out again until the subject was changed or an apology offered.

"One day the hare and his friends were talking about this silly idea of the tortoise. The kindly hare stuck up for him. 'Pray, don't destroy his illusions,' the hare said. 'Consider what a wretched life he leads. Remember his disadvantages. He has had no education. He has seen only about ten yards of the world. He is not a reader, nor a thinker. He cares neither for music nor drama. Art means nothing to him, and his friends are like himself—small-hearted and pigheaded. He lives a cheerless, empty existence—a slow existence in every sense of the word. The one bright spot in it is this grotesque idea that he is such a speedy fellow. Don't laugh at him about it. It isn't kind. Let him go on thinking that he is the swiftest beast that runs. It doesn't do us any harm for him to think so, and it does him a deal of good. If he knew that he was almost the slowest of all beasts and almost the least interesting, he would lose his self-respect, and so his deadly, dull, creepy life would be deadlier and duller and creepier than ever.'

"Some agreed with the hare and some did not, but a rumor of the conversation got to the tortoise and he grew furious. Pity from a giddy, worldly person like the hare was more than he could stand, though he might have been considered pretty thick-shelled over most things. He lost his temper and his judgment. He put an advertisement in the sporting papers challenging the hare to a three-mile run for a bunch of bananas. The winner was to take the bananas and be called Champion Runner of All the Beasts.

"'Now,' said the fox to the hare, 'you've got him at your mercy, and I hope you'll show him once and for all what an old fool he is. You could give him two miles and 1,750 yards and still beat him. I wish you the joy of that bunch of bananas, for win you must.'

"Well, the hare accepted the challenge. He

pretended to go into training and make terrific preparations for the struggle. But in his big, kind heart he had determined to let the tortoise win.

"'You see,' he said to his wife, 'if the poor old beggar crawls home first, it will be the red-letter day of his life. He'll have something to think of forevermore, and you know how long tortoises live. It will brighten up his future and be something for him to boast about and tell his children a hundred years hence.'

"But the hare's wife did not agree. She had no sense of humor, and being a practical doe, she thought it would be foolish to lose a bunch of bananas for a silly sentiment. The hare, however, was firm. He told his friends not to bet on him, because he meant to lose if he possibly could.

"Meantime, the tortoise went into training, too. He got himself into fine condition by eating nothing but clover for a week. Then he asked a friend to time him and found that he could easily go ten yards in five minutes. He considered the victory as good as won.

"All the beasts assembled to see the great race, and from here my story goes on rather like the one you know. Only now you have a different Point of View, and so you understand the tale better than you did until this evening.

"The hare pretended there was plenty of time and strolled about, talked to friends, nibbled a dandelion, and entered into an argument as to whether rabbits or foxhounds could run the faster. Then he sat down and read the newspaper, attended a lecture on the rotation of crops, had a bath, enjoyed his lunch, and took another bath.

"Meanwhile the tortoise was thundering along at the rate of rather more than a hundred yards an hour. He only knew that the hare was behind him, and that was all he cared about, because if his opponent didn't get in front, of course, he couldn't win. The tortoise looked neither to the right nor to the left, just kept forward steadily, day and night. His friends fed him with mustard and cress every half hour.

"As for the hare, he spent a weekend with relations on the other side of the county. From time to time the fox brought him word as to how the tortoise was getting on. The hare had his hair cut, was measured for three new suits of clothes, gave a bridge party, wrote in his diary, took the chair at a meeting to abolish boiled turnips and red-currant jelly, and one morning sauntered down to the starting point of the race.

"The fox trotted up to explain that the tortoise had still fifty yards to finish, so the hare chatted for a few minutes longer, changed his clothes, put on his running drawers and spiked shoes, kissed his family, asked one or two riddles, played a couple of games of lawn tennis with his daughters, and finally started. He ran as slowly as he possibly could and, with the greatest difficulty, by pretending to fall lame, managed to be beaten by a length. And the length was the length of the tortoise, not the hare.

"After the race, the tortoise fainted, only recovering when they played 'See, the Conquering Hero Comes' into his ear. He was pleased, but not in the least surprised at his victory. And that is the end of the true story of the hare and the tortoise."

Among the cheers for the Zagabog, louder than the chirrup of the fairies, came the clear voice of Unity from her seat at the table. "I wonder," she said, "what happened afterward."

"Nothing happened afterward, because that's the end of the story," answered De Quincey, but the Zagabog, whose ears were very sharp, heard the question, and it rather pleased him.

"Human girl," he said, "nobody within my knowledge has ever asked before what happened afterward. I consider it an excellent question, and I shall be delighted to answer it."

The Snick cried, "Hush! Hush! Order for Mr. Zagabog!"

And then the Zagabog continued.

"After the tortoise had won the race and

got back his breath, which took a week, he began boasting and bragging of his amazing victory. He couldn't see for a moment that the hare had let him win out of kindness. But he made so much noise and gave himself so many airs that at last the fox, observing what an ungrateful idiot the tortoise was, thought he might win a little advantage to himself out of it. So he challenged the tortoise to another race for five pounds and a champagne lunch. Much to his joy, the tortoise instantly accepted. 'If I can beat the hare, I can beat the fox,' he said very grandly. 'He may just as well give me five pounds and order the champagne lunch and be done with it.'

"Now we know what the hare's Point of View was when he let the tortoise win, but the fox took quite a different Point of View — a much more usual one. His rule in life was to get all he could out of everybody always. He never allowed himself to consider other people's feelings. You see, there was no poetry or nobility about the fox's mind. He was not a gentleman at heart, but merely a smart fox of business. When they gave the signal to start, he started, and all the tortoise saw was a streak of cinnamon-colored light with a white tip behind it, like the lamp on the end of a train. Before the tortoise fairly got into his stride, he was told that he might stop and go home and order the champagne lunch, because the fox had won. So, you see, when the human girl asked to know what happened afterward, she asked something that was quite worth knowing."

The Zagabog smiled at Unity, and she smiled back, and the fairies made more fuss than ever about her, finding that she was clever as well as beautiful.

Then there was a whisper that the time had come for the ices, but before they arrived, the Snick, who, though perhaps a little vain, was highly conscientious, hurried up to the Zagabog and whispered in his ear, "Pardon me. You've forgotten the moral."

The Zagabog seemed a bit sorry to be reminded about the moral, but he knew the Snick was right, and so he called for silence and told the assembly the moral of his story.

"The moral, of course, is that you must always try to see other people's Point of View before you criticize anybody. Histories are crammed full of unkind things, silly things, and untrue things—why? Because so often the people who write them will not try to see or feel any Point of View but their own. And so our good, amiable hare has been quite misunderstood for thousands of years — and the tortoise, too. False history has been written about them, just because nobody knew the Point of View. So mind that you always look out for the Point of View and help people to see yours, too, if you want them to understand you."

Unfortunately, nobody paid much attention to the moral, except Charles and De Quincey and the King of Fairies. And even they soon ceased to think about it when the ices came in.

A Sad Tale and
a Happy One

⌒ After the ices, Ship, who was not interested in them, came and pulled on Unity's
flower-petal dress and, sorry to say, tore it
rather badly. But it was very late, and he was
remembering the time better than the children. So Charles inquired of De Quincey
whether he might be permitted to ask the
Zagabog his question now. De Quincey asked

the Snick, and the Snick asked the Zagabog, and the Zagabog said, "Delighted." He was always ready to oblige a human boy.

So Charles walked up to the head table, bowed politely to the King and Queen and the Zagabog, and then told the story of how his father had changed. He explained about the meeting and about the gift and asked if the Zagabog would be so kind as to decide what the gift should be.

"What is your father's name?" the Zagabog asked.

"Billy Jago, please, sir."

"Look up William Jago," the Zagabog said to the Snick.

The Snick bowed, rose, and hurried to a large pile of bright-red books in a corner of the hall.

"The Snick is consulting my volumes

of *Who's Who*," explained the Zagabog. "I am told that an earthly volume that goes by the same name is woefully incomplete. The excuse is that they never put in anybody who is not somebody. But that is no excuse at all. Everybody is somebody and I challenge anybody to deny it."

The Snick turned to the *J*s and found William Jago. Then he brought the volume containing Billy's doings to the Zagabog, who read it and shook his head sadly.

"That rascally friend of mine the Thunder Spirit — what a hotheaded boy he is! To think that Phutt and Fum . . ." Here he broke off. Everyone waited in silence, for they did not know what the Zagabog was talking about. At last he shut the book and gave it back to the Snick.

"It is not a case for a gift," he said to

Charles. "On the contrary. You mustn't give your father anything. You must take something away from him."

"Oh, dear," said Charles. "He won't like that. He never parts with anything now."

"He need know nothing about it," said the Zagabog. "In an old waistcoat of your father's that hangs on a nail in an outhouse at Merripit Farm there is a Flint Heart. Get rid of that and all will be well."

"Thank you very much, sir," said Charles. "And I should like to say how much my sister and I are terrible obliged to you and everybody. We bid you all good night, and if ever it is in our power to do anything for the pixies, I hope they'll tell us what it is."

"Capital!" said the King.

"Nicely spoken," said the Queen.

Then Unity, just as she was being led away

by the fairies to put on her own frock again, said very loudly, "I wonder if I might kiss the Zagabog?"

The Snick was clearly shocked. "Hush!" he said. "I hope to goodness he didn't hear you! The Zagabog never kisses anybody, and only very great people are allowed to kiss *him*. Even then only the tip of his little finger."

But the amiable old Zagabog had heard Unity, and he said, "Come here, human girl, and kiss me."

Unity went to him, and the Zagabog picked her up in his hairy arms and kissed her. She looked into his green eyes, and they were like a pair of the most wonderful telescopes, through which she beheld all the past and all the present and all the future at once.

She didn't understand what she saw, but even the little she did understand helped make

her the cleverest girl in all of Dartmoor when she grew older.

So the great night came to an end. De Quincey bade Charles and Unity and Ship a friendly farewell, and his Secretary said the charm outside the Pixies' Holt, so that they were their natural size again, and they set off for home under a night of moonshine and stars.

It was beautiful in the woods, but it seemed so still and cold and lonely that they began to get rather low-spirited before they reached Merripit. Charles tried once or twice to speak cheerfully, but he felt a lump in his throat. So did Unity and so did Ship — though, between ourselves, quite possibly the lump in *his* throat was only because he'd eaten too many good things at the party.

An owl hooted and the sound was so horribly sad that Unity broke down altogether and sobbed. "I won-won-won-won-won-wonder," she said, "if we couldn't go back and ask the dear Zag-zag-zag-abog to let us live with him instead of Father."

Charles braced himself up and tried to comfort her. He didn't understand why they were miserable, but actually it was the most natural thing in the world. After an extra-good time, nine people out of ten feel a little bit miserable — especially if they know the extra-good time is never coming back again.

But they were about to meet somebody who was more miserable than themselves. They were near another farm when Ship rushed into a hedge and began barking fiercely.

A voice cried out, "Spare me! Don't — don't make any more holes in me or I shall be utterly done for!" It was a strange wheezy voice — rather like ginger beer overflowing from a bottle.

Charles called Ship to heel. Then he and Unity went to the hedge and found a mournful

but exceedingly odd and unexpected object
there. Its body was oblong and pale pink. It
had legs and arms about as thick as straws,
and its nose was screwed on to the rest of its
sad face. This nose was round and made of

brass, which glittered in the moonlight. The unhappy thing supported itself on one arm, and they could see that there was an ugly hole in its side.

"Who are you?" asked Charles.

The amazing object sat up. "In a word," he said, using several, "I am an india-rubber hot-water bottle. I was made in Germany and sold in London to an elderly lady who suffered from cold feet. I always went to bed with her and warmed her toes. She came to Dartmoor last year and stayed in yonder farmhouse. How she came to leave me behind, I'll never know. She must have lost her senses. At any rate, it was not my fault. I was in perfect working order at the time."

He sighed and continued. "When the new family moved in, the farmer's wife perceived my virtues. Even her husband the farmer did not disdain to avail himself of my company on cold nights. In fact, I always went to bed with them. They had no children and you might almost say that they adopted me. But I had a weak spot that proved my ruin. On that fatal night — undoubtedly the coldest night of the year — I was fuller than usual with hotter water than usual and I burst. I burst! I would have warned them if I could, but there was no time to do so. They had both just gone off to sleep when a hideous rent in my side flooded the bed with water about one degree less than the boiling point.

"With language I will not repeat, the scalded farmer bounded from his bed, seized me by the throat, opened a window, and hurled me forth into twenty degrees of frost. No one has come to my rescue. I live here — if one may call it living — while the mice nibble

me, the birds peck me, the thorns stick me.
I implore you! Carry me back to civilization
with you if you have any hearts."

Here the poor wretch rose and fell upon
his knees before them. Ship kept pulling
at Unity's dress to come on, but she had a
kind heart. "I wonder," she said, "if we could
mend you."

"You might," he said. "You might try."

"Come, then," said Charles, and the water
bottle, with a gurgle of thanksgiving, collected his remaining strength and leaped into
the boy's arms. He soon complained that the
position was uncomfortable, so Charles folded
the poor soul in two and stuck him in his
pocket. Then he and Unity and Ship set off
running for home.

Waiting in the yard were their father and
John. Mr. Jago cuffed Charles's ears until they

were red. Then he opened the stable door and thrust him in. Next, I'm sorry to say, he whipped Unity and pushed her into the stable as well. He locked them both in and told them they need not expect any breakfast, dinner, or tea the next day. Meanwhile, John had cruelly kicked Ship into his kennel. After that, father and son went back to bed. Billy Jago told his anxious wife that the children had returned and were locked up in the stable.

Though Charles and Unity felt rather sad about this harsh welcome, they didn't mind too much, because they knew that their Point of View was good.

"Tomorrow," said Charles, "we will get the Flint Heart out of Father's waistcoat. Once it has gone, everything will be all right." They curled up against the old cart horse and slept with their heads on its stomach. As for the poor old ruin of a water bottle, he felt the genial glow of Charles and it reminded him of the good old days.

"Warmth—warmth—there is nothing like warmth after all," he said. Then he, too, slept, dreaming of his pride and importance in the happy past, when he was sold for seven and six and began life by bringing joy and comfort to an elderly lady.

The next day Mrs. Jago persuaded her husband that Charles and Unity, who had had no breakfast, should be allowed to come to dinner. None of the grown-ups, including John, believed a word of Charles's story, even though it was quite true. Of course, Charles said nothing about the Flint Heart and the waistcoat until the next meeting, at which he explained what must be done and introduced the water bottle to his brothers and sisters.

Soon afterward, when nobody was about, Charles located the old waistcoat. He couldn't help feeling excited when he put his hand into its pocket and touched the cold, hard face of the Flint Heart. He examined it to see that there was no mistake, then slipped the charm into his own pocket.

Of course, Charles knew what a dangerous thing he had. He felt as if he were carrying dynamite or some equally explosive substance. But to get the Flint Heart from his father was one thing; to get rid of it was another. He decided to speak to Unity in private, and he found her watching the ducks in the nearby river.

Charles shouted at her, "Come here and be sharp about it!"

She was astonished at his tone of voice, but came at once.

"Don't stare," he said. "Just listen to me and speak sense, if you can. I've got the Flint Heart in my pocket. What shall I do with it?"

"I wonder . . ." she began, but Charles was so irritable and unlike himself that he took his small sister by the shoulders and shook her. Ship happened to be passing by, and he could not stand this, so he came toward Charles, baring his teeth and growling.

"You cur!" cried Charles, and he picked up a great stone to throw at Ship.

Then Unity said, "I wonder if you hadn't better fling away that Flint Heart before it makes you any worse."

Charles struggled against the horrid heart and at last dragged it out of his pocket and flung it away with all his might. It landed on the river, but it was flat, so it skipped across the smooth water, jumped the bank, and landed in a reedy swamp on the other side.

"So much for that!" cried Charles. "It's gone and it'll trouble nobody anymore. Forgive me, Unity. You, too, Ship. What a brute of a thing it is."

"I wonder," said Unity, "what you'd have been like if you'd kept it very long."

"I should have gotten worse and worse."

"I wonder how the hot-water bottle would have liked it."

"I'm sure I don't know," answered Charles. "He's better as he is — though as he's so low-spirited, it might have done him good."

"I wonder how De Quincey would have liked it."

"It would have made him rather conceited. He would have ordered others around and

very likely got into trouble with the King and Queen."

"I wonder how the Snick would have liked it."

"The Snick was quite important enough without it," said Charles. "As a matter of fact, I shouldn't be surprised if he's got one."

"I wonder how the Zagabog would have liked it."

"Oh," said Charles, "it wouldn't have made any difference to him. If he'd had a string of Flint Hearts around his neck, they wouldn't have made him unkind."

As they were speaking, Billy Jago appeared beside the river. Unity was about to flee, for the children never faced their father now if it could be helped, but Charles took her hand.

"Don't go," he said. "Trust the Zagabog. If he was right, then Father will be the same good old father he always was now that the Flint Heart has gone." Charles called to Ship, who was sneaking off under the hedge, and all three walked boldly to meet the master of Merripit Farm.

The first thing Billy Jago did was pick up Unity, rub his bristly yellow chin against her cheek, and kiss her. She had not been kissed since the Zagabog had kissed her, and she looked into her father's eyes and saw not telescopes showing the past, present, and future but a very kind, gentle expression.

"Well, my little purty, tibby lamb," he said. "Have 'e come for to meet Father and fetch him home to dinner? And a ride you shall have for your trouble, so you shall."

He carried her on his arm, and with great rejoicing they all went home together.

When Mrs. Jago saw them coming,

she called to Mary, "Oh, my Guy Fawkes! Be that Father carrying Unity, or have my eyes gone 'mazed?"

"It's Father. He's carrying Unity, sure enough, and he's making jokes by the look of it, for Charles be laughing fit to crack his cheeks."

Dinner was late and Billy Jago didn't mind in the least. The family all stared at him as if he were a stranger, but the happy truth was that the stranger had gone and the real, kind, laughing Billy had returned.

John (we have mentioned that he was grown up, haven't we?) seemed the only one who was a little bit sorry, for since Billy had possessed the Flint Heart they had quite got on in the world. The only bright side was that Billy had put quite a lot of money into the bank, but Mrs. Jago felt that, after all, though money is useful, it isn't as useful as a kind-hearted husband.

Billy was changed in every way. He stopped cheating his neighbors; indeed, he apologized to everyone he had been unkind or rude or rough to. He didn't make nearly so much money, but he made more friends. Whatever he may have thought about it, there was no doubt what Mrs. Jago and the children thought. None of them cared a bit about money and were only too glad to have the head of the house back again instead of the grumpy monster that had taken his place.

Only one sad thing occurred at this time, and the sorrow was felt by none but Charles and Unity. It concerned the hot-water bottle and how he might be mended.

The water bottle wanted Charles to send him back to Germany. "I do not wish to suggest that you couldn't mend me beautifully, Charles. I have every confidence in you and Unity. But I have suffered internally in many ways. It is a complicated case, and I shall require the most careful handling if I am ever to be restored to health and usefulness."

"But," said Charles, "it's quite impossible to send you to Germany. I don't even know where Germany is. We will do our best for you. We can do no more."

"Do your best, then," he said with his sad, wheezy sigh.

They tried gum, sticking plaster, stamp paper, glue, and even sealing wax, which hurt the bottle horribly but he bore it without shedding a tear. Yet all these things only made the hole in his side worse, if anything, and at last he begged the children to make no further experiments.

"I can stand no more," he said. "Let me hang on my nail in peace. Go on your way and be happy and forget me for the present."

Charles and Unity tried to do what he told them, but they did not forget him, which is quite fortunate indeed, for though you might suppose that a broken-down hot-water bottle was really not likely to be of any great use again, you would be quite mistaken to think so. In fact, we should never have brought him into the story if we had meant to leave him hanging forever and ever on a nail in the corner of a dark stable.

Still, he must hang there for a little while, just as the Flint Heart must lie in the bog by the river for a little while. But one thing you can count on: the bottle and the Flint Heart will meet before you or they are much older.

A Second Visit to Pixies' Holt

⟡ About six weeks after Billy Jago got well, Charles decided to visit the Pixies' Holt again. He didn't expect to see a fairy, but he wanted to thank De Quincey and tell him how splendidly the Zagabog's advice had worked. So he wrote a very nice letter addressed to Mr. De Quincey, Esquire, Poet and started off to fling it into the hole, where he felt sure someone would find it and take it to De Quincey.

It was August, and the bluebells were dead and gone, their places taken by foxgloves. When Charles arrived, the first thing that he saw was De Quincey himself, trying on a fox-glove hat.

"I was just bringing you a letter," said Charles.

"You ought to have brought it sooner," said De Quincey. "However, better late than never. I suppose I am the last person to expect gratitude from a human boy. If, however, you should ever be invited to dinner again, remember to *call within the week*."

"I will, and I'm sorry," said Charles humbly. "I didn't know better."

"You can't say more, and it is remarkable

to hear you say as much. Many people are angry when they make a mistake, but very few people have the sense to be sorry."

"I hope the music of English prose is going on well," said Charles politely.

"Don't talk about it," said the fairy. "The ancient fires still burn, of course, but there is no fresh fuel, if you understand me."

Charles didn't, so he changed the subject. "My father is quite recovered, I'm sure you'll be glad to hear."

"The King wants to see you," said De Quincey, showing no interest in Billy Jago.

"The King?"

"Yes," answered De Quincey. "The story is a long one, but with my command of the language, I shall proceed to unfold it. Observe the sentences and the harmony with which each will flow out of the last."

"I will if I'm clever enough," said Charles.

"In a word, when you flung away the Flint Heart, it finally reposed upon a bank of wild asphodel beyond the river. Passing that way by night, the Jacky Toad known as Marsh Galloper chanced upon the charm, and with that low cunning denied to no member of his species, he perceived its terrific qualities, possessed himself of the Flint Heart, and, by its aid, lifted himself to a position of intolerable importance. He has marshaled all the legions of the Jacky Toads in revolt against Fairyland; he has openly defied and flouted the Reigning House; his trumpets have sounded for revolution; and his banners bear these shameful words: *Down with the Veto.* Even the Royal Jacky Toad Bodyguard is on the point of rebellion."

"I'm very sorry there is trouble," said Charles.

"Already we have fought three pitched battles, and it is idle to pretend that we got the best of them," continued De Quincey. "Marsh Galloper was practically unknown until a month ago, but now, with his friend Fire Drake and the Flint Heart to help him, the wretched hobgoblin is proving a very ugly customer indeed. Something must be done. So the King wants to see you. His words were, 'Send for Charles.'"

"I'm afraid that I shan't be any use," said Charles.

"Probably not," said De Quincey, "but as the Zagabog used to say, 'Everything comes in useful once in a hundred years,' and this may be your chance. He has, of course, gone on his majestic rounds—I mean the great

Zagabog — but after the third battle, when about six of our leading generals had been recalled in disgrace, the King sent a message by wireless telegraphy to the Zagabog, who is now in Timbuktu, and the Zagabog has replied. The King is very anxious that you shall hear what the Zagabog said."

"I shall be most interested."

"Come on, then," said De Quincey, reducing Charles to fairy size in a twinkling, whereupon Charles realized that all the flowers were arranged in rows and danced on spiders' threads in a way quite invisible to a full-size human being.

"Good gracious," he said, "you're having a flower show."

"Quite the contrary," said De Quincey impatiently. "It's washing day."

In the entrance hall Charles stopped again,

entranced by the loveliest music he had ever heard. This time when he asked what it might mean, De Quincey showed less impatience. "It is the private royal orchestra rehearsing," he said. "They're about to run through a little thing of mine."

"I should like to hear a song of yours if it's half as beautiful as your song about the Zagabog."

"It is more beautiful, but not so learned," said De Quincey. Meantime the orchestra, which had apparently been waiting for De Quincey, stopped playing. After a few words from him, they took up their instruments. A tiny lady songstress took her place before them. After a few opening bars, she sang a song in two very poetic verses about the fairies dancing in the moonlight among the bluebells — bluebells tinkling a fairy tune.

"There," said De Quincey when she finished, "what do you think of that?"

"It's lovely," answered Charles. "Far and away the most beautiful song I've ever heard, though of course I've not heard many."

"Never qualify praise," said De Quincey. "It's the best thing you ever heard. No need to say more."

"Do let me hear it over again," Charles begged, but De Quincey refused to allow this.

"Encores never take place at a rehearsal," he said. "Besides, we must not keep the King waiting."

The King shook Charles's hand and treated him with great kindness. He was not so vain as De Quincey and not so pleased with himself. In fact, his manners simply smothered De Quincey's.

"You are very welcome," the King said, "though I'm afraid you cannot help us as much as you would wish to. Mr. De Quincey will have told you what has happened."

"Yes, Your Majesty. He told me that the Jacky Toads have rebelled against Fairyland."

"True," said the King. "They are led by a powerful and, I fear, unprincipled person called Marsh Galloper. The case is so serious that I sent a message to the Zagabog. If you will allow me, I will tell you what he says." The King then summoned the Reader-of-Dispatches, and while they waited for him, he said, "The Jacky Toads want to abolish the veto, and for my part, I should be disposed to let them try it—as an experiment, you understand—but the Prime Minister won't hear of it."

Then the reader arrived and read the Zagabog's message.

"In reply to your telegram, I have consulted my
Who's Who and so gathered all particulars
of the Jacky Toad Marsh Galloper. His
education has been neglected, and it must begin
immediately. But first you will have to catch

him, and this can only be done with the help of
three things:

1. A human boy
2. A human girl
3. A hot-water bottle made in Germany

When found, leave the rest to them.
Hoping this reaches you, as it leaves me at
present. I remain, my dear King, your friend
and well-wisher,

ZAGABOG"

"Now," said the King, after his reader had
bowed and departed, "you see exactly how I
am placed. We want first a human boy who
will help us, second a human girl who will help
us, and third and last a hot-water bottle made
in Germany who will help us. I have not the
pleasure of knowing any human boys or girls
but you and your sister, and I do not know a
single hot-water bottle made in Germany. But

if I can get you and Unity to help me, that at least will be very satisfactory for a start."

"We shall be only too proud to help you, I'm sure," said Charles.

"So far so good, then. 'Well begun is half done,' as the proverb says. That leaves the great question of the hot-water bottle. It is here that our difficulties will begin."

"Fortunately, I know a hot-water bottle," said Charles. "In fact, you might say that he is my friend."

"Be careful!" murmured De Quincey. "It is a most unlikely thing that you are telling us."

"I promise you it's true," said Charles. "You can come see him for yourself, if you like."

"But not made in Germany?" said the King. "Surely not made in Germany?"

"He really was, King—he said so himself," declared Charles. "Unity and I saved him from a terrible fate and tried to mend him. He is badly wounded, but very cheerful, considering."

"Would he help?" asked the King. "Personally, I would prefer not to engage a foreigner; however, you have heard what the Zagabog says."

"I'm sure he will help," said Charles. "He will do anything he can because I tried so hard to mend him. Besides, he was only *made* in Germany. He came to England at once afterward. The bottle has lived all his life in England."

"A naturalized subject. So much the better. Then everything is comfortably settled," said the King. "I have perfect confidence in you, your sister, and the bottle. After you have restored peace and order in the kingdom, you may all come to Court, and we shall have one of our great nights. Your sister shall choose ten courses of the banquet and you shall choose ten. The audience is ended."

The King bowed to Charles and shook hands again. Then De Quincey began to lead Charles away.

"But," cried Charles, "please tell me what I am to do. I know nothing about it yet."

The King seemed surprised, even a little bit hurt. "You surely cannot have listened to what the Zagabog said. After minute directions, he adds these important words: *When found, leave the rest to them.* So there you are. I have found you and I shall leave the rest to you. The secret of my success as a king, Human Boy, has always been that I find the right fairy for each task and then don't interfere with him. Am I not right, De Quincey?"

The poet bowed. "Quite right, Your Majesty."

Then as De Quincey was once more about to lead Charles backward from the royal presence, the King himself stopped them.

"One thing I must command," the King said. "Please see that the famous 'Night Piece' is sung to Charles before he departs. It is the greatest charm we have against naughty night fairies and night creatures in general. See that he has it by heart before he enters upon his dangerous undertaking."

So when they had gotten outside the hole, De Quincey mounted a pebble under a fern frond, and Charles sat down on an old upturned acorn cup while De Quincey sang the song, written, as he explained, by a poet named Robert Herrick, who after Shakespeare, knew more about pixies than anyone.

This is the song that he sang:

THE NIGHT PIECE

I. Her Eyes the Glow-worme lend thee,
    The Shooting Starres attend thee;
    And the Elves also,
    Whose little eyes glow
    Like the sparks of fire, befriend thee.

II. No Will-o'th'-Wispe mis-light thee,
     No Snake, or Slow-worme bite thee,
     But on, on thy way,
     Not making a stay,
     Since Ghost there's none to affright thee.

III. Let not the darke thee cumber;
     What though the Moon does slumber?
     The Starres of the night
     Will lend thee their light,
     Like Tapers cleare without number.

Charles was greatly pleased with this magic song. He learned it quickly and promised that he would teach it to Unity if he could. He did not forget to say that he thought that De Quincey was a very fine singer, and he was. Though to himself he thought that one might have better liked De Quincey's singing and all the other clever things that he did, had he not made such a fuss about them.

Then, full of the great deeds that awaited him, Charles started for home. His mind was so busy with thoughts of Marsh Galloper and the Jacky Toads that he quite forgot that he was still no more than fairy size. He remembered all too quickly when a great kestrel hawk, mistaking Charles for a mouse or a lizard, swooped down, and if Charles had not screamed, the hawk might well have fixed her sharp claws on him and carried him off for supper.

He rushed back to the hole as fast as he could. De Quincey, who had also remembered and was therefore waiting for him, reproved Charles rather sharply for his stupidity before restoring him to his natural size.

After which the boy set off for home in earnest. That night he told Unity what they had to do, and the next morning they told the water bottle. He was nervous, as usual, but left himself entirely in their hands.

The Galloper

Jacky Toads can be seen only at night, so Charles and Unity knew that they would have to sneak out to the swamp after dark if they hoped to find Marsh Galloper. But what should they do once they found him? Unity wondered if kindness would do any good, and the water bottle hastily agreed that they should try kindness first, but Charles felt pretty sure that when it came to Jacky Toads, kindness would be a waste of time.

"He wants to abolish the veto, and the Prime Minister won't let him. I don't know what a veto is or why the Galloper wants to stop it, but it looks as though the King has made up his mind to support the Prime Minister, so when we do meet Marsh Galloper, the first thing will be to tell him so."

"We must break it to him gently," said the hot-water bottle. "We should say that we are very sorry to disappoint him but that the veto can't *quite* be done away with *yet*, but perhaps, if he'll be good and say that he's sorry, it might *presently* be eliminated."

"No," said Charles firmly, "I shan't do that. I shall let him begin and see whether he is friendly to us or not."

"I wonder how we shall know him when we do see him," said Unity.

"We shan't know him," said Charles. "I've only twice in my life seen a Jacky Toad and they all look alike. They come out in the bog on warm nights and jump up and down like flies flitting over the water. Their lights are dim and strange—not so bright as a night-light and rather bluer."

"Are they dangerous?" asked the bottle.

"Of course," said Charles.

"Then I wish you'd go without me," said the bottle. "I haven't the nerve for this sort of thing right now."

"You must come. The Zagabog mentioned you. Besides," Charles said kindly, "Unity and I will sing the song that De Quincey taught me; no doubt it will protect us."

The very next dark, warm night, the three

of them set out for the great bogs. It was a treacherous spot, but Charles knew it well, and Unity trusted Charles. However, as soon as the poor hot-water bottle's feet touched the mud, he asked to be carried, so Unity picked him up. Then she and Charles sang Robert Herrick's song.

Just as they finished singing, no fewer than four Jacky Toads waved their lights in different parts of the bog. They were little tongues of dim flame, and they flickered up slowly, then stopped and flickered down again. One lantern was nearer and more brilliant than the rest, and forgetting the danger, Charles and Unity dashed forward together.

"Good evening, Mr. Jacky—" But Charles got no further than that, for suddenly he found himself going down, down into an icy cold mire. The mud gurgled and guggled and sucked at his legs as if it were alive. Indeed, the whole bog was shivering and chattering and shaking in a very uncanny and horrid manner. Charles got his arm around Unity, who held tight to the hot-water bottle, and in a few moments, they were safe on a tussock of rushes, above the quaking bog that had nearly swallowed them. The bottle screamed with terror and clung so fiercely to Unity that he nearly choked her, but his screams were nothing compared to the shrill, rude shout of laughter from the Jacky Toad.

"Be gormed if I didn't think I'd got the pair of ye!" The shout came from a tiny, hideous monster, less than three inches high, hairy as a spider, with eyes like rubies and metallic blue wings. The glass of his lantern was blue as well. Charles could see that he was sitting on the skull of a horse on which he put down his lantern and held his sides as he rocked about with glee.

Charles was furious at the vulgar little wretch who had nearly drawn him and his precious sister, not to mention their invalid friend, into a deadly quagmire from which it would have been almost impossible to escape. "Don't think that we are in the least afraid of you!" he cried. "You're a cruel little coward to try to drown me and my sister."

"Yer right," said the Jacky Toad. "You'd both a bin drownded in another minute."

"Of course we would have. What I want to know is why did you try to do it?"

"Blamed if I can tell ezacally," said the imp. "'Tis my business to get you humans into a mess in these here bogs."

"Then it's a horrid business. We never hurt you, did we?"

"Can't say as you did."

"We never spoke an unkind word about you, did we?"

"Not as I've heard tell on."

"I wonder how you can be so wicked, then," said Unity. As the Jacky Toad had no answer to this, he prepared to change the subject, but just then in the blue light from the lantern, Charles saw that the Jacky Toad wore around his neck the Flint Heart—now shrunk to fairy size.

"Why, you're Marsh Galloper himself," Charles said.

"That be my name, though how the mischief you found it out I can't tell."

"By that thing around your neck."

"I wonder if you wouldn't be happier without it," said Unity.

"No, no!" he answered. "'Tis a bit of magic, and it's made me the King of Bog Land. Soon it'll make me King of Fairyland!"

"Treason!" cried Charles. "You ought to have your head chopped off for talking like that."

"You can't chop off a Jacky Toad's head, or its tail either," the Galloper said saucily.

It seemed time now for Charles to change the subject. "I understand," he said, "that you want to abolish the veto."

"So I do," answered the imp, "but that's not all. I want to abolish everybody and be on top of everything, and I'm going to do it." With that he waved his lantern about and began to sing an ugly, discordant song.

The children took the chance to confer. They still didn't know what to do; in fact, it was the hot-water bottle that came up with the course of action. He screwed off his brass nose and handed it to Charles, whispering so that the Jacky Toad could not overhear.

"The Zagabog specially mentioned me, didn't he? Yes, he specially mentioned me. Now I know why. I alone can catch the Jacky Toad."

"Catch him? D'you think we ought to catch him?" Charles whispered back.

"Yes, that is the first step. He will not listen to reason while he is free."

"But how?"

"Take me and pop me over him. The Zagabog must have known that the only cage that will hold him tight is a hot-water bottle made in Germany—leastaways that's how I read the situation."

"We could try," said Charles, amazed at the sudden and unexpected bravery of his friend.

"I wonder if he'll bite you," whispered Unity.

The bottle sighed. "It will not be the first time. But I am doing this for the good of the cause. Now, waste no more time or he may hop away and we shall lose him."

So Charles took the bottle in one hand and the brass nose in the other and began to creep toward the singing Jacky Toad. He couldn't help but worry about the hole in the bottle's side. He'd mended it after a fashion with sticky paper, but would it prove strong enough to make a prison for Marsh Galloper?

"You're whispering," said the Galloper suddenly. "That's ruder than me. What are your names, if I may ask?"

"My sister is called Unity and I am called Charles, and this—"

Here he broke off, made a fierce grab, and brought down the bottle with its rubber lips over the Jacky Toad. Marsh Galloper, finding himself caught, rushed about, scratched and bit and kicked and screamed for his friend Fire Drake to save him, saying such wicked words that Charles swiftly screwed on the bottle's brass nose so that Unity should not hear them.

As for the hot-water bottle, he clasped his hands over his poor stomach and bore the pain of the Jacky Toad as bravely as he possibly could. "All for the good of the cause," he kept saying, and this thought comforted his sorrow as it has often comforted the sorrow of other great heroes.

Having now caught the Jacky Toad, the three of them hurried home as fast as they could go. It seemed cruel to hang the bottle up on his usual nail and leave him with Marsh Galloper tearing about inside him like an angry mouse in a trap, but there was nothing else to be done that night. The bottle took it bravely, begging Charles and Unity to go to bed, but to return as early as they could the next morning. As they left the stable, they could still hear him saying, "It's all for the good of the cause. It's all for the good of the cause."

Early the next morning Charles got up and rushed to the stable.

"Hush," said the bottle, putting his finger to his lips, "don't wake him, for goodness' sake. I've had a truly dreadful night. Indeed, I'm more dead than alive. When the cocks began to crow, the monster finally grew quieter, and about the time your grown-up brother John came to fetch the horse, it fell asleep. How long this will last, I can't say. Nor can I say how long I shall last."

"The first thing," said Charles, "is to get the Flint Heart away from him. Then we shall see what kind of person he really is. Now, bottle, if you're ready, I'll screw off your nose and pull him out."

"Then put on a pair of those heavy gloves. If you don't, he'll bite you to the bone," said the bottle.

But Marsh Galloper did no such thing. He tumbled out of the mouth of the bottle like a sleeping dormouse. Charles removed the tiny Flint Heart that hung 'round the imp's neck and returned him to his prison.

"Don't worry," he said to the bottle. "That thing won't bite and scratch as it used to. You might even find that without the Flint Heart, Marsh Galloper is quite a pleasant person when he wakes up."

"I doubt that," the bottle said. "In any case, I hope the fairies will reward me richly for all I've done."

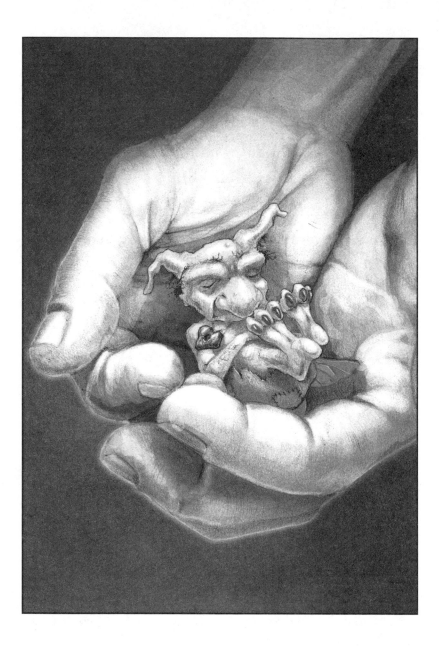

"The least they can do is to mend you," said Charles. "I feel very hopeful that they will when I tell them how brave you have been."

"You put new life into me when you say that. Mind you, I don't ask for the impossible. At my age, one is perfectly contented to be secondhand, but if they would mend me and polish me up generally and make me watertight and self-respecting, however, I have no hesitation in saying that such a concatenation is too good to be true."

While the bottle was using all these absurdly long words, the Flint Heart was beginning to return to its usual size, and Charles was wondering what he had better do with it.

"If you take my advice," said the bottle, "you'll fling it into the beech wood. Nobody will find it there, and soon it will be covered up with leaves and forgotten."

So Charles, very foolishly, did as the bottle suggested and hurled the Flint Heart into a thick wood that rose behind his father's farm. After breakfast he set off for Pixies' Holt with his good news.

De Quincey's secretary was there at the entrance waiting for him. After the Secretary had reduced Charles to fairy size, he handed him a letter from the poet. It ran as follows:

My dear Charles,
The good news of your performance last night
has reached the Court this morning, and you
will be glad to hear that the Jacky Toads, on
losing their leader, have surrendered and begged
for mercy. The King has decided to forgive
them, and the Royal Jacky Toad Bodyguard
has resumed its duties. However, Marsh
Galloper may not return. He will probably be

deported or thrust out of his native Bog Land forever. This dreadful sentence should have been passed by the King an hour ago, but the Queen, whether wisely or unwisely, I will not pretend to say, pleaded with His Majesty to think twice before signing the decree. It is now decided that Marsh Galloper be left in your hands for the space of a fortnight. If, during that time, you and your sister can teach him a few things worth knowing and improve his character, his language, his manners, and his political opinions, then he may perhaps be allowed to return to his friends.

We much regret to hear by secret messenger that you flung away the Flint Heart again. No respectable bird, beast, fish, or other creature is safe until the horrid thing is destroyed. Do not suppose that you have done any good by flinging it away. We shall hear of it again only too soon.

I remain, my dear Charles, with kind remembrances to Unity and the dog Ship, your friend,

DE QUINCEY

P.S. I have not attempted to introduce the magic of English prose into this letter because I find myself in a great hurry and you wouldn't appreciate it in any case.

P.P.S. The King talks of making me an O.M. This is the greatest honor you can get in Fairyland — much better than being created a duke or an earl or anything of that kind. The letters O.M. stand for Observe Me! and if I get them, I shall have them embroidered on all my coattails. I hope you will notice them when next we meet.

"Mr. De Quincey seems as much pleased with himself as usual," said Charles.

"Yes," said the Secretary, "he's making a name for himself. He's so busy running about reciting his poems that he hasn't any time to write new ones."

"I'm glad to hear the King is going to turn him into an O.M.," said Charles.

Much to the boy's surprise, the Secretary shut one eye and tapped his nose with his left forefinger. "Bunkum," he said. It was the first time Charles had ever seen him show a spark of feeling.

Then the Secretary reversed the charm, and Charles left for home. He rather thought that the fairies might have educated Marsh Galloper themselves. Still, it was a great compliment that such a business should have been left in his hands.

First Charles had to see what the pupil already knew, and the next thing was to see what Unity and he himself knew. He ran over his own information on the way to Merripit and was somewhat depressed to find that it did not amount to much. Of course, Unity knew even less, being only five and a half.

The two of them went to the stable to talk

to the Jacky Toad and were astonished to find the bottle and Marsh Galloper in friendly conversation. An immense change had come over the Galloper. He was humble, contrite, and ashamed. At first Charles thought he must be pretending, but this was not so. Since the Flint Heart had been taken from him, the Jacky Toad had begun to improve in every way.

Unity got a box-style mousetrap. Charles half filled it with wet bog moss, then told the Jacky Toad to go into it while he explained the situation.

"The other Jacky Toads have all said they are sorry and have been forgiven," said Charles. "The King meant to deport you, which means you would never have been allowed to go home again, but he has changed his mind. He said that if we can make you clever enough and improve you enough in a fortnight, you may be allowed to return home. But you will have to pass an examination."

The Jacky Toad wrung both hands with grief. "My poor wife!" he cried.

"Dear me! Have you got a wife?" asked Charles.

"'Ess, a wife, but no other family except my wife's niece, who lives along with us under the root of a bog bean. Us never had no trouble till I picked up that thicky dratted stone. Then I got a lot of nonsense in my noddle and went fighting the other pixies and here I be—driven from my home and no hope of getting back."

"There is hope if you will set to work and learn all we can teach you," said Charles.

"You can't larn me nothing. I'm a born fool, that's what I be, else I wouldn't be sitting here catched in a mousetrap."

"I wonder what you do know," said Unity.

"Naught—only a few things about the bog I lives in. That's no good."

"You must know something about the Veto, at any rate," said the bottle, "because that's what you were fighting for."

"Good," said Charles. "He must know that."

"Be gormed if I do," said the Jacky Toad. "You got to fight for something, if you go fighting at all, so I fought for that. But what 'tis I haven't a notion."

"Then how did you find out there was such a thing?" asked Charles.

"From a newspaper. Some fisherman left it down by the river. My friend Fire Drake's a bit of a scholar and he read out *Down with the Veto*. So I thought us would shout the same."

"Well," said Charles, "as you know nothing, we must begin at the beginning. I shall teach you arithmetic and history and the kings of Israel. My sister Unity will teach you sewing, embroidery, and poetry—as far as she has got herself."

"And I," said the hot-water bottle, "will give you lessons in geography, of which I know more than you might think."

"I wonder if you'll learn enough in a fortnight," said Unity.

The Galloper shook his head sadly. "You'll

get me pretty well muddled up among ye," he said.

"Yes, yes," said the bottle. "There's the danger that if you try to teach him too much, he will burst somewhere, as I did."

"I wonder what we'd better leave out," said Charles.

"Sewing," suggested Marsh Galloper.

"Anything else?" asked Charles.

"The kings of Israel," said the Galloper. "I'll have a dash at the rest, though goodness knows whether my thinking parts will stand it."

The lessons began the following day. They found a large cookie tin for the Galloper to live in while he was being educated. Every second day they gave him fresh bog moss and every evening half an old marmalade jar of wet mud. Still, two things troubled him. He could not light his lantern, and he could not write a letter to his wife. They tried to cheer him by saying that if he worked hard enough, he would soon know enough to write her. This did not comfort him in the least, because, as he explained, even if he did write to her, she couldn't read it.

And here the chapter ends, but there is one small thing to mention before we go on, so that it won't interfere with the next chapter.

It happened that just about this time, the bottle asked Charles and Unity for a favor. "Everything has a name," he said. "I think I ought to have one also. I shall feel more important then."

They quite agreed with him and asked what he would like to be called.

"Something to remind me of my homeland," he answered. "Of course, by my homeland I mean Germany, where I was made. How would Potsdam do?"

"I don't like the sound of it," said Charles.

"May I be called William, then?"

"That's my father's name."

"How would Bismarck do?"

Charles agreed to this. It was a rather large name for a humble hot-water bottle out of repair, but nobody was hurt, and he never brought any discredit upon it so far as we know.

The Examination

 We won't bother to say much about Marsh Galloper's schooling, because you know perfectly well what goes on at school and what uphill tedious work it can be. Besides, you cannot exactly say that Marsh Galloper was at school, because there were no other scholars. It takes more than one Jacky Toad to make a school, just as it takes more than one swallow to make a summer, or more than one currant to make a plum cake. It would be more correct to say that Galloper was at a "crammer's." Indeed, he had three crammers, and they crammed him with all their might and main. So night after night, the poor fellow went to his wet moss with a splitting headache after plastering his forehead with fresh mud to cool it. Had you been there, you might have heard him as he tossed in his sleep saying, "London is the capital of France"; "Twice five are four, twice six are nine, twice seven are fifty-three"; "Mary had a little lamb, its fleece was black as jet, and everywhere that Mary went, the lamb you also met"; and so on—which showed he was learning steadily, but without much system.

The teachers, as I said, did their best, and as the time approached for the examination, it was necessary to keep Marsh Galloper up with extra doses of liquid mud. Bismarck taught him by night, Charles gave lessons in the afternoon, and Unity made him learn poetry and do embroidery in the morning.

At last the great and grand day of the examination arrived. The water bottle professed himself too nervous to attend, and Unity wondered if it might be better if she stayed at home and held his hand, while sending up a prayer or two on behalf of their pupil. So Charles carried Marsh Galloper to the Pixies' Holt in an old tobacco tin and handed him over to the Fairy Commission waiting at the entrance, who, we regret to say, were too caught up in the excitement of the day to think clearly. They rushed the Galloper into the Examination Hall, totally forgetting that a human-size boy would be helpless to follow. Charles called after them, hoping someone would hear and send a pixie back to reduce him to fairy size. But no one came, and poor Charles, eager as he was to hear the results of the examination, was forced to stay outside the hole and wait none too patiently for word from within.

Soon he noticed that all the nearby birds and beasts were bustling about in a most unusual manner. It was obvious that something quite out of the ordinary was taking place. The birds and beasts were gathering in groups, and what was most extraordinary was how the creatures that usually quarrel at sight — or fight and wrangle at any rate, if they do not actually go further and eat each other — were coming together in a friendly and excited manner all evidently busy about the same matter.

Meanwhile, the Jacky Toad was met with a solemn sight when he entered the Examination Hall. On one side sat the fairies — two or three thousand of them — and on the other side all the Jacky Toads from Marsh Galloper's own swamp. At the end of the hall was a raised platform with gold chairs and footstools, where the King and Queen were seated. There was also a blackboard for the marks that the Galloper might win. And there was, of course, an Examiner Royal. You won't be surprised to learn that the Examiner Royal was De Quincey himself. He had not yet been made an O.M., but he hoped that after his examination of the Jacky Toad, he would receive that honor at once. He wore a cap and gown and looked even more learned than usual.

Somewhat overwhelmed, Marsh Galloper bowed and scraped very humbly and touched his forehead to everybody. Mrs. Marsh Galloper, who sat in the front row of the Jacky Toads, between her niece and Mrs. Fire Drake, cried out loud when she saw her husband, because he was looking so thin and wild and sad. She asked if she might kiss him to give him courage, but this was not allowed.

After a chair was provided for the pupil, De Quincey rose, gathering up a huge bundle of papers from a nearby table.

"I beg to inform Your Majesties," he began, "that we are here to inquire into the education of the late rebel Jacky Toad, known as Marsh Galloper. I have heard from the human boy Charles that the Galloper has become wonderfully improved in his general character, and that, of course, is well as far as it goes. But his fate does not depend on these things. It depends on what he has learned. If he passes the examination that now awaits him, he will be allowed to return home to his wife, his relations, and his acquaintances, but if he fails, then he will be cast out — to be seen again among the people of the bog at his own peril."

Everyone applauded De Quincey for putting the matter so clearly before them. The poet continued. "Our examination consists of arithmetic, history, geography, embroidery, poetry, and general knowledge. I propose, if Your Majesties are willing, to take the general knowledge paper first."

Unfortunately, the Jacky Toad's weakest subject was general knowledge, because neither Charles nor Unity had any worth mentioning and so couldn't teach him. But the bottle knew a thing or two, and Marsh Galloper determined to do his best.

"My first question is this," began De Quincy, examining his papers, "what's a freemason?"

Marsh Galloper frowned and looked at

the ceiling, then at the windows, and then at his toes. "I can't tell 'e, because I doan't knaw," he said.

"You don't know! Very good — or, I should say, very bad. Your Majesties, I ask you to observe that the prisoner at the bar does not know what a freemason is."

"A freemason," the King explained to his people, "is a mason who has not joined the trades union. Now, go on."

De Quincey took a piece of chalk and wrote a big 0 on the blackboard before asking the next question. "What is a categorical imperative?"

"Never saw one, so I can't say," replied the student.

De Quincey shrugged his shoulders and wrote up another big 0.

The Jacky Toads all began to get anxious, and there was a good deal of whispering.

"You will observe, Your Majesties, that the prisoner has never seen a categorical imperative," said the Examiner.

So the King, with his usual good nature, explained it. "They occur in the woods with the other members of the fungi family during October and November," he said.

Everybody cheered, and De Quincey asked another question.

"Is the moon or the sun more important?"

"The moon," answered the Galloper instantly.

"Wrong."

"The moon's the most important to me," said the Galloper.

"*You*—you're nobody," said De Quincey.

"I'd soon show whether I was nobody if I got you in my bog!"

The King interrupted the argument. "Put up one mark to the prisoner," he said. "He was perfectly right to say the moon, because from his Point of View, it *is* the more important. I must ask you all to remember what the dear

Zagabog said on the subject of Points of View when last he dined with us."

So De Quincey put up a mark, though with very ill grace.

"We now proceed to arithmetic," said the Examiner. "I should like to know the prisoner's opinion of five times six."

"Twenty-nine."

"Wrong." De Quincey put up another big 0.

But the King made him rub it out again. "He was so very nearly right that he may have full marks all but one," he said.

The Jacky Toads cheered loudly, and De Quincey wrote up four marks.

"If you multiply three by four, divide the result by two, subtract one, add seven, and then multiply the total by twelve, what's the answer?"

Of course the Galloper had not the

slightest idea; nor did anybody else in the hall for that matter, but he felt he should make a stab at it. He knew that twelve times twelve, which was the highest number he had reached, was one hundred and forty-four, so he thought that would do as well as anything and said it.

"Right!" answered De Quincey and put five marks on the blackboard. But when the immense cheering died down, the King spoke up. "It is a perfectly magnificent answer. I could not have replied more correctly myself," he said. "So put up one hundred marks at once."

Naturally, De Quincey had to obey, but as five was full marks, it rather muddled up his arrangements. "There will be no more arithmetic," he said rather shortly. "I shall now proceed to history. My first question is, where did Julius Caesar land?"

"At Plymouth," answered the Galloper,

since Plymouth was in Devon and thus the only seaport he had ever heard of.

"Wrong." De Quincey chalked up a big 0.

"Wait!" said the King. "As a good Devon pixie, I ask if you are *quite* sure he is wrong?"

"Quite, Your Royal Highness. It is believed that Caesar landed at Deal."

"Well, *I* believe that he landed at Plymouth," said the King. "He was a clever man, and he would never have made a mistake of that kind. Full marks for the Galloper."

A cheer rewarded the King for this clever correction of history. De Quincey chalked up five marks. But he didn't like it.

"My second question occurs in the reign of William and Mary. What does the prisoner know of Mary?"

"Mary had a little lamb," Marsh Galloper instantly replied.

"That's wrong, at any rate," declared De Quincey. "You're mixing up poetry with history."

"Well," said the King, "even if he is, he's not the first person to do so."

"Of course, if Your Majesty is satisfied—"

"Perfectly," said the King. "Let's go on now to something else. I never much cared for history—except, of course, the history of my own kingdom."

"We now come to embroidery," said the Examiner Royal. "As I don't pretend to know anything of that subject, I must ask Your Majesty to call a jury of needleworkers."

"No need," said the Queen. "I will decide the point."

Everyone clapped their hands, and the Galloper produced his piece. Under Unity's direction, he had worked a tiny sampler on a whortleberry leaf. At each corner was a star with six points, and in the middle were the words *Bless Our Home.*

The Queen examined the work carefully. "A masterpiece," she said. "I will keep it."

"Her Majesty honors the Galloper by keeping his sampler for her own use. Treble marks!" said the King.

When the applause had ceased, and Mrs. Galloper had been calmed down, for she was growing quite hysterical with the strain, De Quincey took up the next paper.

"Geography," he said shortly. In fact, his speech was getting shorter and shorter, and he felt really in a rage. But you can't be in a rage before the King or you will get into trouble, so he hid his feelings as well as he could.

"Geography is my own favorite subject," declared the King. "A good deal will depend upon the answers to this section."

But a thought struck the Queen. "It is tea-time," she said.

"Then the examination is suspended for half an hour," said the King. With that he and the Queen rose and retired to their private apartments. A great clatter filled the examination hall. Some of the crowd were full of hope for the Galloper, but others, looking at the long line of 0's, merely shook their heads. When the royal pair returned, some in the crowd noticed that the King took with him his own *Manual of Modern Geography*.

The Jacky Toad Fails

ᘯ "Our first question," began De Quincey. "What is the size in square miles of the United States of America?"

There was no use to even try to answer that. "I doan't knaw at all," Marsh Galloper said.

"Mark that, Your Majesty. He doesn't know *everything* after all," said De Quincey rather snidely.

"Of course he doesn't," said the King. "Who does? Excepting the Zagabog, of course. Next question."

The Examiner marked up a big 0 and proceeded. "What is the difference between a peninsula and an isthmus?"

"That's a riddle," said the King. "I won't have riddles asked at a serious time like this. Next question."

"What is the difference—?" began De Quincey.

"I tell you, I won't have it!" said the King.

"Well, then, what does the prisoner know of volcanoes?" said the Examiner, feeling a bit like a volcano himself by this time.

"Excellent question," said the King.

Unfortunately Marsh Galloper knew nothing about volcanoes. The King frowned and the hearts of all the Jacky Toads sank.

"For the benefit of my subjects in general, I will say that Etna, in Sicily, is the largest in Europe for the moment. But you never know what may happen. Dartmoor was a volcano once. Proceed."

But we can't tell you much more about the geography paper, because it is too painful. De Quincey kept asking questions, and the Galloper couldn't answer any of them. A fearful row of big 0's appeared on the board, and at last the Galloper, in a voice of anguish, cried out, "May it please Your Majesty, let me ask *him* something for a change."

"Ridiculous nonsense!" cried De Quincey. "Who ever heard of a person who is being examined asking the Examiner a question? Such a thing never was known to happen, Your Majesty."

"Because a thing never happened is no reason why it never should. Let us be broad-minded. Besides, it is absurd to suppose that the prisoner, who has been learning geography for only a fortnight, can ask you anything you don't know."

"Of course it is."

"Then let him go ahead."

Marsh Galloper was quite ready to do so. "What be the names of the six grand duchies of the German Empire?" he said.

"A capital question!" exclaimed the King, taking a peek at his manual.

But De Quincey frowned, coughed, blew his nose, curled his whiskers, and then laughed and said, "What an extraordinary thing. They have quite slipped out of my memory for the moment."

"Ask him another," said the King.

"What do 'e know of Baden?" asked the Galloper.

"Baden?" said De Quincey to gain time.

"'Ess, Baden."

"Well, let me see — tut-tut! On the tip of my tongue, too!"

"So were the answers to all your questions on the tip of my tongue. But I couldn't manage to get 'em off," said the Galloper.

There was a great shout of laughter at this point, but it was not wise to make public fun of a great poet-pixie for long, so the King provided the information that Baden was a famous resort in Germany and announced that the geography examination was ended.

"The last subject is poetry," said De Quincey, quite humbly. "Is it Your Majesty's wish that I examine the prisoner in poetry?"

"Yes," said the King, and added with his usual tact and kindness, "we well know that on the subject of poetry you stand first in our kingdom."

De Quincey bowed at this compliment and continued. "It seems to me the simplest plan will be not to ask you what you don't know, but to find out what you do."

"Bravo!" said the King. "The very essence of the Examiner's art. Proceed."

The Galloper put his paws behind his back and recited several nursery rhymes flawlessly, but the last one ran into a bit of trouble. It went as follows:

> "Little Miss Muffet
> She sat on a tuffet,
> Eating her curds and whey,

When there came a great hornet,
And played on his cornet,
And frightened Miss Muffet away."

"Wrong!" De Quincey was just about to put up another big 0 when the King gently stopped him.

"You are quite right to say that he is wrong," began the King, "but perhaps, in actual practice, it would not much matter whether Miss Muffet was alarmed by a spider or a hornet. Her terror and flight are the dramatic point of the poem, and whether it was the rudeness of a spider sitting down beside her without an invitation or the stupid practical joke of a hornet in suddenly sounding his cornet close to her ear appears to me to matter but little, but if I am mistaken, please correct me."

"Your Majesty is perfectly correct," said De Quincey. "I had not looked at it in that light. It is a variation of the classical version, but there may be authorities to support it. And, as you cleverly point out, the result to the heroine is the same."

"In any case," declared the Queen, "variety is charming."

"Go on then," said the Examiner to his subject.

"I doan't knaw any more," said Marsh Galloper, "but after Unity teached me these, I made up a bit of a rhyme myself. It ban't very clever, but I just mention it to show how terrible hard I have tried."

"Repeat it," ordered the King, "and let nobody laugh."

So the prisoner recited these words:

"Shall I never see my own Marsh again,
And the hole by the old bog bean?
Must I leave my wife behind,
Who was always good and kind?
Shall I never see my own Marsh again?

Shall I never see my dear friends again,
And the skull of the old dead horse?
Shall I never wave my light,
So blue and queer and bright,
From the skull of the old dead horse?

Shall I never suck the beautiful mud
That abounds at my little front door?
Shall I never hop and dance
And sing and leap and prance?
Shall I never see my Marsh anymore?

Shall I never —?"

"Stop!" ordered the King. "Not another verse. I couldn't stand it. The poem is too sad. Not another verse."

In fact, the King need not have ordered nobody to laugh. It would have been more to the point if he had ordered nobody to cry, for the Jacky Toad's poem had brought tears to the eyes of many in the company. As for Mrs. Marsh Galloper, she cried so bitterly that the Queen sent the poor wife her own bottle of smelling salts by one of the young princes.

"The form is crude," declared De Quincey, "but the sentiment is haunting. It may have full marks." He chalked up five for the Galloper's effort and then said, "The examination is now concluded and I shall count up the marks. The maximum is two thousand seventy-five, and the minimum is eighty. I much fear that when the big zeroes are added up and subtracted from the marks, we shall find the prisoner has not succeeded."

A great silence fell on all while De Quincey did his calculations. At length he shook his head. "Alas!" he said, and I think he was really rather sorry. "Seventy-eight naughts from one hundred thirty marks leaves only fifty-two marks. The prisoner has failed."

A deep groan burst from Fire Drake and the Galloper's friends. Mrs. Galloper fainted and had to be carried into an antechamber.

Galloper himself fell on his knees, lifted his clasped hands to the King, and fixed his ruby-red eyes on the royal countenance.

The King put on his eyeglasses and calmly looked at the blackboard. "Pardon me," he said, "and if I am wrong, correct me, but I think you are mistaken. How many naughts do you have there?"

"Seventy-eight, Your Majesty."

"If I am not gravely in error," said the King, "seventy-eight naughts come to nothing at all. You will not deny that naught is nothing. That fact is known to everybody."

"You are misunderstanding me, Your Majesty. In this case, however, it is not for me to bandy figures with my sovereign—"

"Then let us ask for a second opinion," said the King. "Send for Charles!"

When Charles, now reduced to fairy size,

of course, was ushered in, the King greeted him kindly and explained the problem.

"Tell me, Human Boy, how much are seventy-eight naughts? Don't answer in a hurry. I think one thing, my Examiner Royal another. We are both content to abide by your decision."

A great silence fell while Charles considered. At last he spoke. "Seventy-eight naughts are . . . nothing, Your Majesty."

A roar of applause shook the Examination Hall, but the King had his trumpets sounded for silence. "Half the problem is solved, but now we must subtract the seventy-eight naughts from one hundred thirty marks. You may make your calculations on the blackboard if it would be easier."

Charles felt no need for the blackboard. "Seventy-eight naughts are nothing," he said.

"Subtract nothing from one hundred thirty, and one hundred thirty remains."

"But—but" said De Quincey, "each of those naughts signifies a bad mark. They are not *really* naughts. In my mind they stood for—"

But the King was quite worn out. "The Examination is ended. We cannot go into the question of why a naught is not a naught. That is a problem for your poetic mind. As King, I cannot permit myself any of these fancy arguments. Marsh Galloper has got one hundred thirty marks. He has passed. Release the prisoner and tell him to be in my Audience Chamber at five o'clock tomorrow morning to kiss hands in a token of forgiveness."

Amid a great hubbub Galloper rejoined his wife and friends, and, screaming with delight, the legions of Jacky Toads returned to their marsh.

The King then turned to Charles. "If you'd like to take us as we are, without ceremony," he said, "Her Majesty and I shall be delighted to entertain you at dinner."

But Charles felt it would not be fair to Unity and Bismarck if he did this. He explained to the King that the others would be terribly anxious to know the outcome of the examination.

"Of course they will," said the King, "and as the credit is theirs also, we must have you all to visit us. I shall not forget. You will receive an invitation in a week or ten days. In the meantime, I shall consider whether some little appropriate distinction may not be dispensed to all three of you. Perhaps the fourth or fifth class of my Royal Titanian Order would meet the case."

So Charles, with many thanks, sped off,

full of the good news. But excited though he was, he could not fail to notice that things on the moor and in the woodlands were not as usual. Some remarkable event had upset the birds and beasts—by now even the reptiles and insects were stirred up. He thought Ship might know why and determined to ask him as soon as possible.

Mr. Meles
and the Deputation

Needless to say, Unity and Bismarck were
delighted at the triumph of Marsh Galloper.
Unity wondered what the fifth class of the
Royal Titanian Order might be, but she was
overjoyed at the thought of visiting Fairyland
again. The bottle was, of course, very anxious
to go, with the hope that he might be mended,

which would mean much more to him than a compliment from the King.

So they waited for the invitation to come, but it did not. Strangely enough, it was Ship who told Charles the reason for this. You'll remember that since their first visit to Fairyland, they could understand each other.

"There's a dickens of a row on," said Ship in his rough-and-ready dog language, "and it's all the badger's fault. He's been ordering people about and insulting everybody. He says he *will* be obeyed and declares that the whole moor belongs to him."

"It sounds to me as if he's found the Flint Heart," said Charles.

"Exactly," said Ship. "You flung it into the wood, and he was in there poling about after pignuts, came upon it, and took it home to amuse the children. But very soon he found out how strong and fierce and powerful it made him. So he kept it, and he's getting stronger and fiercer every day. He'll soon be master of the moor if something isn't done."

"Is that what all the beasts are meeting for?"

"Yes. They have had fifty-seven meetings and appointed a committee. The committee, which consists of the fox, the pheasant, the owl, the grass snake, and the chief beetle, has decided on a Deputation."

"I wonder what that is," said Unity.

"It is a solemn thing," explained Bismarck. "It consists of a number of people who come to some great person to tell him that a number of other people want something very much. He listens attentively to what they say and promises to think about it seriously. Then he thanks them for coming and the deputation withdraws. That's about it, generally."

"The beasts intend to have their Deputation right away," said Ship.

"What great man are they going to?" asked Charles.

"To the King of the Fairies, of course. They have given him notice that they are coming on Thursday fortnight. The Public Hall in Fairyland is being readied for them."

"That will be such a tremendous business that I'm sure the King can't invite us until he's seen them and got it off his mind," said Charles.

In the meantime, Mr. Meles the Badger, who until he had found the Flint Heart had been a very modest creature, got the idea that all the meetings going on were in preparation for crowning him King of the Beasts.

"They know I shall give nobody any peace until I am crowned," he told his wife and children. "They will have to admit that I am the most important of all creatures."

Mrs. Meles sniffed.

"They are gathering and having large meetings every day. I expect them to arrive with the crown at any moment."

Mrs. Meles sighed behind her paw. She was feeling just as Mrs. Phutt had felt, just as Mrs. Billy Jago had felt, and just as Mrs. Marsh Galloper had felt. Which showed that the Flint Heart was almost worse for the wives of the creatures who found it than for the unfortunate things themselves.

The great day of the Deputation arrived, and it was the largest deputation on record.

As a rule, a deputation does not exceed twenty or so, but this deputation was five hundred beasts strong and two hundred yards long. They walked in pairs, like the animals into the ark (that is, all but the fleas, who rode in), and they represented every creature that lived on Dartmoor.

De Quincey had kindly dashed off a marching song for the occasion. To hear them singing it with one voice as they tramped forward by hill and dale, through streams and over the tors, would have been a great treat.

When they finally arrived and entered the hall, six spokesmen, who had been selected with great care, stepped forward to present the case to the King.

They had chosen the fox for his cleverness, the hedgehog for his common sense, the heron for his oratory skill, the owl for his wisdom, and the dor-beetle because he was an orphan.

The King nodded to his acquaintances among the creatures, shook hands with personal friends, and bowed to the entire assembly. Then, having an excellent memory for faces, he noticed that a well-known beast was missing.

"Where's the badger?" he asked. "Where is Mr. Meles?"

"Well may you ask, Your Majesty," replied the fox. "Where, indeed, is the badger? It is on the very subject of the badger that we five hundred beasts, birds, reptiles, and insects have come before you in solemn deputation today."

"Can it be possible that he has annoyed you all?" asked the King.

"Every blessed one of us, Your Majesty," replied the hedgehog.

"How extraordinary!" said the King. "I have known him for years, and a better-tempered, better-hearted, less cranky gentleman I never wished to meet."

"He has sadly changed, Your Majesty," said the heron. "We are here to tell a dismal tale of his downfall and —"

"If Your Majesty pleases, you had better listen to the deputation," interrupted the owl, who well knew what a terrible talker the heron was once he got started.

"That is what I am here for," said the King. "Do begin."

Whereupon the fox stood up, consulted his notes, and opened the proceedings. "The badger," he said, "has decided to become King of the Beasts. We have decided that he shall not be anything of the sort. He is by no means the kind of person to turn into a king. He is plain and ignorant. He is narrow-minded and a bad sport. He eats the partridges' eggs and uses exceedingly vulgar language. He scratches and bites everybody and behaves in a most unkingly manner. We are, in fact, sick and tired of his bluster and bullying and

horrid ways and feel that something ought to be done."

Then the hedgehog got up. "As a practical beast, I know that the badger is doing a great deal of harm and unsettling the young people and filling their heads with nonsense. He wants them all to make him king, and if they do, he has promised to divide the moor among his followers. It isn't his to divide! I object to this ridiculous way of going on and feel that something ought to be done."

Next the heron rose to have his say. "As representing the feathered legions of the air, I have to announce our rooted and fixed determination never, under any sort of temptation, to yield our allegiance to the badger. We owe him no thanks, we are not in his debt, and inasmuch as he has taken to eating eggs, it will appear to all beasts and birds assembled that the feathered legions of the air cannot be expected to gaze with a kindly eye on this ill-favored and nocturnal creature."

Here the owl interrupted. "There is no objection to his being nocturnal. I am nocturnal myself."

The heron merely looked shocked at being interrupted and went on. "The question appears to me and to the feathered legions of the air, in whose interest I now appear, to lie under seventeen heads, or divisions. I shall proceed to examine each of them so that we may see how we stand and what course we ought to pursue."

"Pardon me," said the King. "It would give me great pleasure to hear you examine the seventeen heads of the question, but there really won't be time."

The heron bowed, trying without success to conceal his disappointment. He had hoped to make a great impression. Sadly, even though he was a fine talker, he always managed to be deadly dull. So he finished his speech, dragging it out as long as he could.

"In that case, Your Majesty, I will content myself with saying that not only I but those feathered legions of the air, which I have the honor to represent on this occasion, feel that something ought to be done."

When the heron sat down at last, the owl stood up. "Something *must* be done," he said. "It is a case for deeds, not words."

This was a dig at the heron, and the King and Queen could not help smiling a little, but they applauded the fine brevity of the owl.

Although the frog was not one of the chosen spokesmen, he had been hopping about in his eagerness to be heard and couldn't help speaking up. "If there is one person here who has more right than another to speak," he said, "it's me. Meles has eaten both my grandmothers. Two kinder, gentler, harmlesser old ladies never lived. And now they are gone. They have been taken from us by this abominable murderer. We shall never see leg of them again. Nobody is safe. Death is let loose among us, and who can tell whose turn it may be next? In a word, something ought to be done. If nobody else will do anything, I will risk following my grandmothers and tackle the badger myself!"

All cheered the frog for his fine fighting speech, and there was not a dry eye among the reptiles when he sat down again.

After him the beetle seemed very tame. He mumbled something about being an orphan and about having had to fly for his life from the badger on several occasions, but nobody, I fear, paid much attention to him, for the Deputation wanted to hear what the King would say and even more to know what he would do.

"There is little doubt—" he began, but a curious noise at the main entrance caused him to break off and listen. "There is little doubt—" he repeated, but the noise increased. People don't often dare to make a noise when a king is speaking, and naturally he was annoyed by it. "There is little doubt—" he said for the third time when he was quite silenced by a regular din and hubbub. Several official fairies rushed to still the clamor.

"There is little doubt—" resumed the King, but now his speech ended altogether, for there was a violent rush from the entrance.

The Jacky Toad guards were sent flying in every direction, and who should appear but the badger himself.

"It's beastly of you all—simply beastly!" he cried. "I won't have it!"

He wore a tweed suit, a bowler hat, and a loud green-and-red tie. The Flint Heart dangled about his neck like an eyeglass, and he carried an umbrella that he waved over his head in a violent and impertinent manner.

"Take your hat off!" said the King. "How dare you make this vulgar noise when I'm speaking?"

"I didn't know you were speaking," said the badger, "and I shall not take my hat off."

"Why not?"

"For the simple reason that I am a king myself," replied the badger. "One king doesn't take off his hat in the presence of another. We're equals."

"My dear Meles," said the King. "You must be mad. How can a simple commoner suddenly blossom out into a king?"

"He can when he's clever enough. If you knew history—which you evidently don't—you'd jolly soon see that all sorts of people have become kings. You've only got to be man enough."

"Remove his hat," said the King quietly, "then I'll sentence him. This is no case for argument. A pretty king he would make."

A regiment of Jacky Toads rushed forward, surrounded the badger, knocked off his hat, and took his umbrella away. The indignant beasts all shouted at the badger.

The King then addressed the badger with great kingly dignity. "I have no wish," he said, "to be unreasonable or exercise my power in an unkind manner. I will content myself with explaining to you that you are wrong. Before anybody can become king over anybody else, one of two things must happen. The person must either follow some other member of a royal family to the throne, or he must prove himself so brave and clever and wonderful and powerful that the people with one voice proclaim him king and invite him to put on the crown—even insist upon his doing so. Well, the other beasts have not the slightest wish to make you their king. They used to like you—as I did myself—but now they do not. In fact, they dislike you very much, and it is all your own fault, because, to tell you the truth, you are not brave or clever or wonderful or powerful. You are merely a very badly behaved and ignorant badger who has given a great deal of unnecessary trouble and done a great many very wrong and foolish things."

"Oh, shut up!" said the badger.

The King was so astonished that he nearly fell off his throne, but he kept his temper despite this unforgivable insult. "It is you who will be shut up," he said. "In fact, worse than that must happen to you. To interrupt the king is—well—really, I don't know what it is."

Then he turned to his Lord Chief Justice, who wet his thumb, turned over the pages in his enormous *Book of the Law,* and then said these terrible words: "The sentence of the High Court is that anybody Interrupting the Monarch shall be hanged, drawn, and quartered."

"There, now," said the King, turning to the badger. "See what you have done? You will be hanged, drawn, and quartered on the afternoon of Wednesday next. Now, kindly go home and let us hear no more of you until the time comes for the punishment. Then I shall expect you to be here punctually at half past four for the hanging, drawing, and quartering. Be punctual, Meles, I say, or even worse things may happen to you."

At this moment there was another scene at the door, and before anybody could stop her, Mrs. Meles, with her four children, rushed in. They rushed to the steps of the throne and knelt down in a row. Mrs. Meles began to talk, but it was difficult to understand what she said because she talked so fast. In any case, she had come too late to save her husband.

Then everybody else began talking also. Some people, but only six, thought the sentence was too severe. Everybody else thought it was quite satisfactory — or, if anything, too light.

Fortunately for the badger, one of the six on his side happened to be very powerful. The other five wouldn't have counted, because they were his own wife and children. But the sixth was the Queen herself. However, against the Queen and the badger's family were the five hundred beasts, birds, reptiles, insects, the Jacky Toads, and all the fairies, so the King found himself faced with one of the most difficult problems that he had been called upon to tackle for a long time.

After five minutes deep in thought, during which the company kept silence — except the badger himself, who whistled a stupid tune as loud as he could and stamped his feet and rattled his claws and pretended he didn't care a brass farthing for anybody — the King gave an order.

"Send for Charles!" he said in a clear and royal voice.

So they sent for Charles, and this saying of the King's became a sort of sly joke in Fairyland ever afterward. If anybody upset a cup of tea, or broke his shoelace, or overslept, or forgot a message, or took the wrong umbrella, or had a headache, or even hic-cupped, somebody always said, "Send for Charles!" But they took care that the King never heard about it, because as wise and good as he was, he sometimes had trouble appreciat-ing a joke when the joke was on him.

The Sentence

⤳ While it occupied exactly no time for a fairy messenger to reach the ear of Charles and inform him that the King of Fairyland wanted him immediately, Charles, even though he made the greatest haste, took half an hour to reach the Pixies' Holt. But the time was passed quite pleasantly, for, at the King's direction, light refreshments were served to the entire company — excepting, of course, the badger, who had nothing.

When Charles arrived, the King put the case before him. The question for Charles to decide was whether the badger should or should not be hanged, drawn, and quartered. The badger was still in a rude, boisterous frame of mind and pretended he did not care.

"Well, Your Majesty," said Charles, after carefully considering the question, "of course you know best. I can see clearly that the badger has sadly changed, and he deserves a very serious punishment. But, if it was me, I should only carry out part of the sentence."

"Which part?" asked the King.

"I should not hang him."

"Why not?"

"Because it would spoil his usefulness,"

said Charles, "and never give him a chance to turn over a new leaf."

"True."

"And I should not quarter him for the same reason," continued Charles, "but I should certainly draw him, because a badger can be drawn. It often does him good and teaches him humility."

"Capital advice," said the King. "He shall be drawn, and Charles shall draw him."

But with great politeness, Charles explained that it is not boys' work but dogs' work to draw a badger. "I have a friend called Ship, Your Majesty. He was at the splendid party you gave for Mr. Zagabog. Well, Ship couldn't draw the badger himself, because he is a sheepdog, but he has two friends, Flip and Chum, who are fox terriers. They, Your

Majesty, can both draw badgers. In fact, they are famous at it."

"Very good," said the King. "I leave the matter with confidence in your hands." He turned to the assembled beasts. "The Deputation will be glad to hear that Charles and his friends Flip and Chum will draw Meles the Badger on Thursday next, at three thirty of the clock. And now, my dear creatures, I have the honor to wish you all a very good evening."

After the King and Queen had retired, Charles spoke to the badger. "I know quite well what's the matter with you, badger, and I'm very sorry for you. The quicker you let my friends draw you and get that hateful Flint Heart away from you, the better you'll feel."

"Never," said the badger. "The beast or

boy who tries to take it from me shall feel my teeth and claws first. I'll tear him to pieces."

He refused to give his address, but that didn't matter in the least, because the Deputation knew it perfectly well and happily went home as the most successful deputation on record. Charles told Unity, Bismarck, and Ship of the King's decision, and Ship went that same evening to see Flip and Chum to explain to them that they must be ready to draw a badger on the afternoon of Thursday next.

"That's work worth doing," said Flip, who was a shapely lady terrier. "I'm sick and tired of killing rats, and a badger always means a good rousing fight."

"I shall have to go into training," said Chum, who was somewhat stout, "or I shall be too fat to get into the badger's burrow."

As for the badger himself, he was not idle

either. He prepared to make a terrible fight of it, declaring that the fox terrier who could draw him wasn't to be found in the world. So it promised to be a pretty tough battle.

When the great afternoon arrived, hundreds of beasts were already on the scene to see what should happen. They sat in rings, as though it were a circus, and when Charles, Unity, Ship, Flip, and Chum appeared on the stroke of half past three, all the beasts stood up, gave them three cheers, and wished them luck.

The badger felt perfectly certain that neither Flip nor Chum nor fifty such dogs could draw him, but he knew that there would be a terrific struggle, so he had sent his wife and family to her mother's on the other side of the moor. Mrs. Meles wanted to stay and help, but he refused to hear of it. He said that it would not be ladies' work, which was true. He also said that he would undoubtedly kill both of the dogs when they came to draw him, which remained to be proved.

He settled himself in his study at the very end of his holt with the Flint Heart firmly tied around his neck. In the darkness his eyes glimmered like two green railway signals. His claws had been specially sharpened for the occasion, and his teeth were always sharp.

Flip, her eyes shining red, went through the hall, the dining room, the drawing room, and the nursery until she came face-to-face with the master of the house in his study. Behind her, Chum, too stout to get farther into the burrow, waited in the entry hall.

The fight was really dreadful. The badger tore and scratched and clawed and snapped and tugged. Flip bit and worried and gripped and snarled and pulled. Fur flew off both creatures, and both were nearly choked in the fury of battle. Now Flip dragged Mr. Meles into the drawing room. Now Mr. Meles made a tremendous effort and got back to his study again. In the bedlam the ceiling came down, nearly smothering them both, but it forced them out of the study once and for all.

Still the battle went on. Flip was growing weak from loss of blood. The badger
found himself rather feeble as well. But I don't
think he would have been beaten, save for
his enemy's cleverness. Flip, in a very artful
manner, pretended that she had had enough
of it, causing everyone outside to greatly fear
for her, because she set up a fearful yelping
and howling as if the badger were eating her
alive. But really this was a trap. When Flip
started to crawl away, as though trying to
escape, the badger, proud of his great victory,
followed her to the hall, intent on giving her
a parting bite on the nose. Instead, he got a
bite himself. Chum's powerful jaws closed like
a rattrap on the badger's right ear. Then Flip,
knowing that this would happen, got a firm
hold of the badger's left ear, and before the
badger had time to say "Jack Robinson!" he

was trundled out of his house tail over head, upside down, and nearly inside out. When he arrived in the open air, the poor fellow looked more like a worn-out doormat than the great and important Mr. Meles.

The beasts rushed forward, yelling and screaming, and it was all that Charles could do to stop them. So Ship and the big dogs acted as policemen, keeping them off, while Charles did what he could for the combatants. First he looked after Flip, who was very weak and so beaten and exhausted that she rolled over on her side and didn't move for half an hour. But the badger was even worse. He, in fact, had fainted as soon as Flip and Chum had let go of him.

Then Charles, who had brains and knew how to use them, did two wise things. First, he sent a wood pigeon for Mrs. Meles, for if the badger was going to die, she ought to be there to say good-bye to him, and next, he took his knife, cut the string, and removed the Flint Heart from the badger's neck.

As soon as he had told Ship to look after Flip, Charles began to run as fast as his legs could carry him to Pixies' Holt. He knew only too well that the hateful Heart was already beginning to do its work, and he was determined to hand it over to the fairies before it could make any more trouble.

Meantime, the badger opened his eyes. "What's happened?" he asked. "Where's my dear wife?" He appeared to be in a dream and apparently had not the faintest idea of the things that had gone on.

"What has occurred?" he asked. "Who's been treating me like this?"

"You've been drawn," said Chum. "My friend Flip has just drawn you—with a little help from me."

"But why? What on earth have I done to be drawn? A badger's holt is his castle. You were quite out of order to do it."

"You had to be drawn," explained a partridge. "It was your punishment. You've been behaving horribly, bullying everyone you met, and you know it. Didn't you eat my eggs?"

"Eat your eggs! Good gracious, no!" cried the badger.

"Didn't you send me on your errands?" asked the woodpecker.

"Never! I go on my own errands—such as they are."

"Didn't you tell me to move away?" demanded the fox.

"Good powers! No, of course not. I was only too proud to be allowed to reside in the same terrace with you."

"Didn't you say that you meant to be king of us all?" asked the owl.

"King? King? *Me, king?*" Weak and shattered though he was, the idea evidently struck him as so wildly absurd that he laughed till he cried, and the tears made his bitten face smart most painfully.

They calmed him down so that he felt distinctly better before his wife returned. And a few days later, when he was fully recovered, he insisted on going around to all the beasts, birds, reptiles, and insects and apologized to each of them personally. He sent a letter of contrition to the trout and salmon as well. He could do no more than that, and everybody forgave him, except the frog, who I am sorry to say never would, quite forgetting his own motto of "Keep cool whatever happens."

The badger also went to Fairyland and expressed his humblest and deepest regrets. So the King pardoned him and kept him to tea, which was the proudest moment of the poor badger's life and closed the incident.

But we must return to Charles, who had arrived at the Pixies' Holt with his great news. He cast the Flint Heart down before the King and refused to touch it. The King, who was rather scientific, sent for his learned men and had the Flint Heart enclosed in a bell glass. Then they pumped out all the air so the charm lay safe in a vacuum, for the present. But the problem was what step to take next.

"The problem is truly difficult," the King said. "Whatever we do, somebody may suffer. If we throw the charm into the air, a bird will get it and there will be trouble among 'the feathered legions of the air,' as the heron so grandly called them. If we fling it into the river, a salmon will get it, and between ourselves, the salmon think quite highly enough of themselves as it is. If we fling the stone on the earth, we shall have some fresh trouble among the beasts, and if we leave it here, sooner or later some fairy will be sure to get ahold of it, because nature abhors a vacuum, and she won't allow us to keep even the Flint Heart in a vacuum for long. Therefore, the question is, What shall we do with it?"

Before anybody could reply, there came a messenger to the King. "May it please Your Majesty," he said, "the human girl Unity and the hot-water bottle Bismarck are at the door. Unity wonders whether they may come in."

"Let them enter," replied the King. "I have long wanted to meet the hot-water bottle. He may be presented at once. As for Unity, a

Woman's Wit, as I have remarked on former occasions, will often solve a knotty problem when the Profounder Male Mind utterly fails to do so."

So Unity and Bismarck entered the Presence. She had picked up the hot-water bottle on her way, and they had hurried after Charles, hoping to catch her brother before he got to the grove to tell him the good news that Mr. Meles was better and that Flip also had almost recovered at the promise of thirty beefsteaks.

Good-bye, Flint Heart

Ꮼ The King welcomed the visitors kindly
and was concerned to hear of the bottle's
poor health. He sent immediately for five of
the Court Physicians, and the bottle retired
with them to be examined. Charles and Unity
were naturally anxious about Bismarck, but
Unity had to think of the problem that was
set before the King. His Majesty explained the

situation to her and asked if any idea of importance occurred to her mind.

"In a word," concluded the King, "the Flint Heart is a Danger to Society, and I confess that I can't for the moment see how on earth, or under water, or in sky, to deal with the matter."

Unity put her finger in her mouth and frowned, which she always did when she had to think of anything difficult. Then, after a silence of at least ten seconds, she said, "I wonder what the dear Zagabog would do."

Everybody looked at the King, and when they saw him smile, they heartily applauded Unity.

"Woman's Wit," said the King, "has once more conquered a difficult situation. To wonder in Fairyland is to know. We will hear what the good Zagabog would do. Set the wireless telegraphy at work instantly. The Zagabog is on the Riviera—no distance at all. Inform him that the Flint Heart has been captured after a struggle, that it is at present confined in a vacuum, and that the King of Fairyland wants to know exactly what he should do with it." He looked at his watch. "It is now fifteen to six," he said. "We shall get the answer at fifteen to seven, if not before. We will pass the time with a charade or two and a cold collation."

So the message was sent, the charades were acted, and the cold collation eaten. Then came a bright and happy event for Charles and Unity and, indeed, for everybody. The doors of the royal consulting room were thrown open, and the five royal physicians marched out playing a charming little polka on their stethoscopes. And in the midst, radiant and perfectly well, from his bright brass nose to the points of his toes, tripped the hot-water bottle.

He had become a different creature altogether. Instead of being limp and forlorn, dejected and full of holes — an object of pity to the kind observer — he was grown prosperous, stout, handsome, sound, and as good as anybody. His flat face was wreathed in smiles. He walked with a light and elastic tread. He shone all over, and his nose glittered like a star on a frosty night.

He was so excited that he danced and threw a somersault or two, scarcely containing himself for delight. He gave Charles a hand and kissed Unity warmly, for warmth was always his strong point.

The Senior Physician explained that he

and his companions had swiftly discovered what was wrong with the hot-water bottle and cured him while he waited. In fact, as Bismarck himself said, he was as good as new, if not actually better.

The King was much interested at hearing about the bottle's adventures and inquired what his future plans might be. Bismarck said that he had never given them a thought because he considered that his career was as good as ended. It quite upset all his ideas to find himself hale and hearty, thoroughly well again, and "fit for honest work."

"I am fond of work, Your Majesty, and never so happy as when comforting somebody on a cold night."

Then a happy thought struck the King. "You shall stay with me," he said. "In fact, the weather is thought chilly for this time of year.

You shall come to bed with Her Majesty and myself this very night."

The bottle was overcome with emotion. Think what a splendid fortune had overtaken him! One moment he was a poor broken-down invalid, full of holes and misery, hanging by his handle on a nail in a stable, and the next he was cured by fairy physic and not only found himself in splendid trim again but actually invited to sleep with the King and Queen.

Even his voice had much improved, as he broke into song:

"Sing hey! And sing ho! For the jolly hot bottle,
    So soft and so plump and so kind and so warm;
Let the water be boiling right up to his throttle,
    And he'll cuddle by you and keep you from harm.
Sure the King and the Queen
    Will forget all their woes
When the jolly hot bottle
    Is tickling their toes!"

After this capital song, the bottle was led away by the Gentlemen of the Bedchamber to explain to them how his nose screwed off and other things they needed to know. Just as he marched away at one door, after taking an affectionate farewell of Charles and Unity, there entered at another the wireless-telegraph boy with a message from the Zagabog.

The herald opened it and read it to the Court. Thus ran the message:

Hotel Royal, San Remo

To the King's Excellent Majesty, from his faithful friend and admirer, the Zagabog:

In order to safely and harmlessly destroy the charm known as the Flint Heart, take one human boy — the boy called Charles — and one human girl — the girl called Unity. Choose a fine Friday morning before dawn, and bid Unity bear the Flint Heart in her pinafore to the Cuckoo Rock, where my friend the cuckoo always sits to rest when he arrives on Dartmoor for his summer holiday. Then direct Charles to bring the road mender's biggest hammer and strike the Flint Heart thrice. It will instantly become dust. Next the King of Fairyland must fling one pinch into the air; the Queen must fling one pinch into the water; the Lord High Chancellor must fling one pinch upon the earth. All creatures at any time interested in the Flint Heart shall be present at the ceremony, and afterward, the Dawn Wind will sing her song, the sun will rise, and everybody must go home again to breakfast.

Hoping this will find the King and Queen of Fairyland as it leaves me at present. I remain their true friend,

THE ONLY AND ORIGINAL ZAGABOG

P.S. The Snick sends his love and respects.

"Tomorrow will be Friday," said the King, "so why waste a week? Let the order be sent out instantly for all to gather at Cuckoo Rock tomorrow before dawn. Unity will bring the Flint Heart in her pinafore, Charles will bring the road mender's biggest hammer, and his father, Mr. Billy Jago, must be present."

The Flint Heart was taken from under the bell glass by a fairy of science with a pair of magic tongs. And the remarkable thing is that though Unity carried the Flint Heart home, she continued to be just the same little wondering, raggedy robin of a Unity as ever. The charm did not make her the least bit worse than usual. Which shows one of two things: either the Flint Heart knew what was going to happen and began to get frightened and lose its power, or else Unity's own little heart was too sweet and altogether lovely to be troubled by the naughty charm.

The cocks began to crow at four o'clock the next morning, for they seemed to understand, like everybody else, that an important thing was going to happen. The cuckoo, who was late in leaving Dartmoor that year, had just settled himself at the top of his own special stone when he looked about and saw that beasts, fairies, and other people were approaching from all directions. Being a shy bird, he took off and didn't stop flying till he got to France.

The folk from Merripit Farm arrived first — Billy Jago and John, who was grown up, Sally, Mary and Teddy, Frank and Sarah, Jane and the baby, and last, Charles, carrying the road mender's largest hammer, and Unity, with her pinafore held out in front of her and the Flint Heart upon it.

Next came the beasts of importance and,

of course, the badger. Nobody was more interested in this ceremony than he was. Indeed,
when he saw the Flint Heart, he bristled all
over and would like to have ground it into
powder himself. Ship, Flip, and Chum also
arrived. Then came the regiments of the Jacky
Toads, with Marsh Galloper and his wife and
his wife's niece, Fire Drake and his wife, and
many other important members of the clan.
Next appeared the Fairy King and Queen with
the royal family and the hot-water bottle, the
Lord High Chancellor, and other high offi-
cers of the Court, including, of course, De
Quincey, now proudly sporting the O.M. on
his coattails, Hans Christian Andersen the
storyteller, the heralds, the chorus, and the
band. Ten thousand fairies followed, because
the King dearly loved a great pageant and
liked a crowd to see it.

But others had yet to come, for when the company was grouped about the Cuckoo Rock, two dim stern shapes grew out of the morning light and stood huge above the stone where lay the Flint Heart. They were greater than any of those present, and you could see the sunrise through them, for they were spirits from Shadowland. One was Phutt, the terrible chief of the Grimspound clan in the far-off Stone Age days, when the Flint Heart set out upon its career, and the other was that mighty magician Fum, who made the Flint Heart at his mystery shop beside the river.

Vaster still, towering into the dawn, touched with the wild glory of day-spring, ascended two enormous and majestic figures above the ring of the tors and high into the sky. These, indeed, might easily have been mistaken for gigantic purple clouds, fledged and fluted with gold and scarlet along their peaks and precipices and crowned with the herald banners that shot to the zenith of the sky from the coming of the sun. But they were not clouds at all. The fairies and those who understood the truth about things knew very well who they were. And so did Unity, for she waved her sunbonnet and kissed her hand and cried, "I wonder where the darling Zagabog gets his lovely clothes!"

And the King said, "He gets them from the sun every morning, for like myself, he never wears the same suit twice, and as you will observe, they are a perfect fit."

Indeed, the two glorious objects, towering like pillars on either side of the eastern sky, were the Zagabog and his friend the Thunder Spirit, clad in their very best. They were both much interested in the ceremony, and the Thunder

Spirit even forgot to laugh, which is a good thing, because if he had, he would have spoiled the music and alarmed many of the company.

Then came the solemn moment when the Flint Heart was to be changed and administered in small doses to earth and air and water. Charles struck it three times. At the third blow, behold! A little pile of gray dust took the place of the glittering, hard, black flint stone. The King took the first pinch and flung it into the air, and the birds gave a mighty sneeze. The Queen took a pinch and flung it into the river, and the fish became immensely excited and dashed about as they do after a hard spring rain. The Lord High Chancellor took the last pinch and flung it upon the earth, and the beasts coughed and snorted. But the effect upon all the creatures was the same. The dust of the Flint Heart braced them up, making them brisk and cheerful. It acted like a tonic upon every one of them, whether they wore fins or fur or feathers, whether they breathed water or air.

That is the reason why Dartmoor is so stinging and bracing and puts such life into you — why it makes you feel so hungry and so jolly. That is why Dartmoor water is so foaming and refreshing, so cold and brisk, and why Dartmoor earth is so tough and elastic and springy that you can walk or run all day upon it and never grow tired. There is a touch of the Flint Heart still about Dartmoor, and the people who live there still need it. They must be pretty hard and strong and ready for anything up among the high tors and heather, especially when winter comes and the great North Wind spreads his snowy wings and the East Wind shows his teeth.

But it was the gentle Dawn Wind that now ended this ceremony, as the Zagabog had promised. A great silence followed after the last pinch of the Flint Heart had been scattered over the earth and all the beasts had cleared their throats.

Then from the sky there came a murmur of music, wild and soft, and the Dawn Wind sang a melodious and somehow joyful song that the listeners could not really understand, but they were glad because they knew that the Dawn Wind was glad, and they watched her sweep away with the Zagabog and the Thunder Spirit through the wonderful Gates of the Morning.

Then with good heart and good appetite, everybody went home to breakfast.

THE END

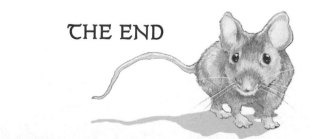